# Living Room

# Living Room

## Allan Weiss

*Nov 10, 2002*

*To Barbara:*
*Thanks, and good luck*
*with your novel!*

## BOHEME PRESS

Edited by Lori McLellan

Text and page design by magpie media/Patricia Cipolla

Previous versions of these stories have appeared in the following
magazines: "Property" (*NeWest Review*, August/September
1993); "All the Birds That Fly" (*The Windsor Review*, Spring
1994); "Minorities" (*The Fiddlehead*, Summer 1992); "Living
Room" (*Short Story*, Spring 1995)

Canadian Cataloguing in Publication Data

Weiss, Allan Barry
Living room: stories

ISBN 1-894498-05-4

I. Title.

PS8595.E4886L58  2001    C813'.6    C2001-930554-0
PR9199.4.W44L58  2001

First published in 2001

Printed and bound in Canada

Boheme Press
110 Elena Crescent, Suite 100B
Maple, Ontario, Canada  L6A 2J1
www.bohemeonline.com

To my parents, Tom and Freda Weiss, for their
boundless love and support

# Acknowledgments

Thanks to the Cecil Street group, especially those members who provided their invaluable comments on these (admittedly non-SF) stories. Their critiques, and our stimulating discussions of and debates on the craft of writing, undoubtedly made me a better writer.

Special thanks to Lori McLellan for her fine editorial work, and of course to Max Maccari for his support, his hard work on my behalf, and his writer-friendly approach to publishing.

# Table of Contents

# Property
====

When I was six years old I knew our street perfectly. For instance, I could tell you where everybody lived by the colours of the doors to their duplexes: Howard Cohen's had blue doors, Paul Wasserman's green with white trim, and the duplex where Daniel Stern and his big brother Gary lived had shiny varnished doors. Paul's duplex had the best dirt under the stairs for making roads, while mine had the best backyard. And since everybody knew where everybody else belonged we all respected each other's property. If someone was an enemy that week, he knew he'd better not step on the wrong side of the street. "You don't live here!" we'd yell. "Stay off our property!"

Fortunately, the lines between our properties were well-demarcated. Goyer Street, with its rows of neatly-parked cars along either curb, separated Daniel and me from most of the other kids I knew, and high wooden or metal fences separated the backyards of those who lived next door to each other. Every backyard and fence was different, in size and look, and we would brag about what we had, or in times of hate make fun of what someone else had. "My backyard is better than yours and you can't come!"

Sometimes I hated everyone, and then I could lie on the grass in my backyard, under the crabapple tree, shielded by ranks of close-standing wooden pickets. From there, the surrounding duplexes were invisible—even those of Barclay, the street parallel to and behind Goyer but high up a steep slope. Barclay's yards, red brick walls, and iron staircases were hidden by the woods running like a spine down the middle of the block.

The yards of both streets abutted onto the woods, but there were no fences on our side, so I considered those woods part of our property. It was my favourite place to play, with or without my friends, and I explored the woods until I knew every tree, every boulder. I called the biggest tree rising straight up out of the slanting soil "my" tree—it was the one I always climbed or played near, and so belonged to me. My mother would sometimes come out of the kitchen onto the back balcony, and yell at me to be careful as I pulled myself up into its branches to sit in the unyielding fork where I dreamed of building a treehouse. I didn't understand why she was worried, so I ignored her as long as I could before finally dropping to the ground to keep her happy.

She even worried when I played up there without climbing my tree, because the ground sloped so steeply. She was sure I'd slip and break my arm; even my father once said at the supper table that he was surprised that hill didn't cause more accidents, although I had no idea what kind he meant. No matter what they said, I'd never give up my woods.

The only kid in our neighbourhood who ignored the rules about property was a retarded kid named Stevie—we never found out his last name because no one I knew had ever spoken to him and he didn't go to our school. No one was his friend, obviously. Daniel managed to scare us by claiming he'd once been to Stevie's house and seen where they tied him to the bed or wall to keep him from breaking things and biting people. I half-believed him. None of my other friends ever claimed to have played with him, and I couldn't imagine anyone trying.

Stevie would stand silently nearby and watch us play, occasionally venturing to within a few feet of us. If you tried to talk to him he'd start to cry and run away. As long as he didn't bother us I could tolerate his coming onto Goyer, even though he lived on Bedford, one street down. But even retarded kids had to obey the law, and as far as I was concerned the laws of property were absolute; they were how things were supposed to be, the way the world worked. I even thought the word property was based on "proper" somehow.

My best friend that summer was Paul. We would squat in the low space under his front stairs and run the sides of our hands through the dirt, smoothing out roads for our Dinky cars. Stevie would stand not far from us, watching us unless the passing of the 160 Bus or a big truck attracted his attention. We could see him peering at us through the sparse hedges that walled the narrow front lawn. For some reason he never came that close when I played with anyone else. I kept hoping God or his mother would take him away from there, but it didn't happen.

"Go away!" I yelled at him. "Get back to your own property!" He'd just stand there as if I'd said nothing, shiny finger between his lips—not so much ignoring me as not understanding. And every day, it seemed, he moved closer to where we were playing, despite warnings, insults, everything we threw at him.

"You should tell your mother," I told Paul once. "He's not supposed to be here."

"I know."

I stood up as far as I could and walked, hunched over, to where I could watch Stevie's movements, steadying myself with one hand on the gritty concrete. By now he was almost on Paul's walk. "Get out of here!" I yelled, but Stevie didn't move. "Go home!"

I ran up to him, fist clenched, and threatened to smash him in the shoulder. For a split second he looked at me with unfocused eyes, his hair sticking up in all directions even though it was really short. Then he burst into tears and ran, clutching the back of his head with both his hands. I waited until I saw him disappear around the corner of Wilderton before returning to my place under the stairs.

"Don't let him come here," I warned Paul, aiming my index finger at his nose.

"I try!" he insisted. "He never listens to me." I recognized the phrase, and even the intonation that his mother often used on him.

I smoothed a new road in the dirt, in the process forming a ridge blocking a cross-street, one that Paul pressed down with his fingers. The first car I tried on the roads was my black police car with the white doors. It was the biggest car I had, and the most elegant as far as I was concerned. I watched a daddy-long-legs scurry by, making sure it was gone into the grass before I continued. "I saw the President on TV yesterday."

"So did I!"

I ignored him.

"He was driving in a car like this one." While watching the news my father had insisted on pointing out the procession of black cars going down some street in Washington. Usually I avoided the news, but the parade was too spectacular to miss. "I mean, it wasn't a police car, but it was black and this big." We had watched the President wave as his car turned down a street, his wife sitting beside him and sometimes waving, too.

"My father said that he's going to be elected again next year."

"Why?"

I shrugged. At the time, I thought that the President was our President; and when I saw Lester Pearson I knew that he was our Prime Minister, although how they governed the country together was not clear. My father had been very happy when Lester Pearson got elected a few months before, and so, of course, was I. "My father also said Kennedy is the best President we ever had."

Paul nodded, and scratched the back of his hand the way he was always doing.

"How are we going to keep Stevie away from here?" He was becoming dangerous; there was no way of knowing what he would do, especially if he was retarded. Paul didn't answer, so I said, "Should we tell on him?"

"Tell who?"

I thought about that but didn't know who would be the right person to tell. Someone had to be responsible for keeping people off your property. In school each day we said the Lord's Prayer, and I remembered the part about trespassing. I knew what that meant, because I'd asked my father after seeing a sign on a silver-painted metal fence that said:

No Trespassing/Défense D'Entrer

No matter what it said in the prayer, trespassing was illegal.

Paul ran my huge, black police car around the complex weave of roads we'd made, and we now pretended it was the President's car, slowly winding its way through immense crowds.

At home I told my mother about Stevie. She was busy washing the dishes, hands covered with yellow rubber gloves and white foam. She said: "Ignore him and he'll go away," giving no more thought to her words than to which fork she chose to pull out of the brownish water and scrub with her thumb.

But Stevie kept coming back, refusing to respect boundaries. I did try to ignore him, and in fact after a while he would go away, but then he'd be back—if not after lunch, then the next day. Once or twice I chased him off again just by coming out from under the stairs; one look at me and he ran. Otherwise, the only thing that kept him from standing there all day was boredom; eventually, he'd run off as if he had somewhere really important to go. But he still had no right to be on our street, and his presence there was, to me, a shocking violation.

He became intolerable the day I finally got to ride on the Borden's delivery truck. I'd just gotten a new Dinky Toy dump truck, with a "dumper" you could actually raise and lower, and rubber tires I hadn't lost yet. We were using it to clear away the dirt from hand-flattened roads when I spotted the white delivery truck crossing Wilderton. I peered out from under Paul's stairs to watch as it rolled slowly down Goyer, stopping at most of the houses. On the side of the truck was a rich painting of Elsie the Cow, almost three-dimensional against the white paint. At each stop the milkman carried a metal basket out of the truck and strode quickly to the porch where two or three empty bottles stood next to the door. He removed the conical note and bills sticking up out of the mouth of one of the bottles and returned to the truck with the other empties symmetrically arranged in the basket. A few moments later he came out of the truck and brought the order, his every step making the bottles clink noisily, and dropped the change into the remaining empty. I walked to the sidewalk admiring the operation, determined that I would be a milkman myself some day.

"Come on!" Paul yelled. "The road's not finished!"

I ignored him and followed the truck, shielding my eyes against the glare off its glossy side. As the truck passed through the long, morning tree-shadows, the sunlight flashed off it like lightning. I pretended it was pushing its way through a violent storm, bringing milk no matter what the danger. When it stood before my own duplex, I ran to look through its open back doors. Gleaming metal racks held hundreds, maybe thousands, of bottles: many of the bottles were empty, but most were full of blue-white milk, with a whiter band at the top, and capped by crimped aluminum foil. Against one wall of the truck stood a huge square stack of butter in rectangular foil packages, the kind we bought, but in uncountable numbers. On the other side were neatly ranked egg cartons, and bottles with yellow caps: buttermilk, my grandfather's favourite. Under all the racks were large sheets of thick, brown cloth draped over blocks of white ice.

Paul stood next to me, leaning on the rugged metal ramp protruding from the truck's end. He ran his lower lip back and forth under his buck teeth. "Get away or you'll get into trouble," he told me, scratching the back of his right hand.

"No, I won't."

I'd long dreamed of riding in the back of the truck with all that milk, all that ice around me. Not to go far, just far enough—maybe to De Vimy at the end of the street. I backed away as the milkman returned, carrying the basket that now held four empty bottles. He looked down at me from under his cap but because of the shadows I couldn't tell if he was smiling or angry. He put the empty bottles into what seemed like carefully chosen places in the racks and went up front. He drove further up Goyer, both Paul and I following closely. After making another delivery, he got behind the wheel, turned around, and said: "Want a ride?" in what I could tell was a French accent.

"Sure!" I said.

Paul and I climbed up and stood in the aisle between the racks. I tried sitting on a ledge of blanketed ice but it was too hard and cold, so I stood up near the back. The truck jolted forward, and I watched the street flow by slowly. I saw the buildings I knew so well scrolling away behind me, holding their cement walks out to me and then withdrawing them.

At the truck's stops, we stood aside to let the milkman deposit empty bottles and pick up full ones. He mostly ignored us—which suited me fine—because it meant he wasn't about to kick us off. Each time the truck started or stopped we held onto the racks or cold walls, and the bottles rattled in their steel racks, but amazingly none shattered or fell out.

We continued down Goyer past Howard Cohen's house, past Gail Moscovitch's, even past Gordie Zeitner's—my worst enemy. The street matched my mental map, but was more interesting, more exciting, seen from the back of the milk truck. Every duplex was divided from its neighbours by square-cut bushes and sharply sloping driveways that ended in garages or stone walls in the middle, with steps leading up to the back-yards. I'd never seen the bushes and driveways slide by this way, at least not without a car window blocking me from them and making them look like part of a TV show.

As we neared De Vimy I felt a jab of fear that I might never get off, that I would be carried up De Vimy, past Barclay, into unknown territory. So when we were just outside the home of Mrs. Dorowitz, my mother's old friend and sometimes our baby-sitter, I hopped off and Paul did the same. We watched the truck turn the corner, then ran back to Paul's house.

When we arrived at Paul's we stopped cold. Stevie was under the stairs, playing with my dump truck! He was rolling it back and forth over the same strip of dirt and making deep engine noises, saliva stringing off his lower lip. He didn't look up at us when our shadows cut across him; he just kept playing, as if it wasn't important to acknowledge our being there, as if he owed us no apology.

"That's mine!" I yelled, grabbing the dump truck out of his hand. He looked up at last, his face twisted into the beginnings of a cry. "Get out of here!"

He started to cry in earnest now, screeching as the tears rolled from his eyes. Paul pushed him in the back, which only made it harder for him to get up and away. "Get off our property!" Paul ordered, but Stevie just sat there, crying. I'd never seen anything like it: the world's rules meant nothing to him; he was incapable of following them, like every monster I'd ever read or heard about.

I stood over him, fist raised, and growled, "Go home, Stevie." He cried for a few more seconds, then, exhausted, got to his feet and began running. As he passed me I swung at him, landing a punch on his shoulder.

Paul and I chased him down Goyer and around the corner onto Wilderton, running as fast as we could but not really trying to catch him. We chased him around again to Bedford, right to his house, where he raced up his stairs and fell backwards against the front door, one hand clutching the knob. We stood on the sidewalk, not daring to step foot on his walk, because we knew the rules.

"REE-tard! REE-tard!" Paul chanted, and I joined in.

Stevie began to cry in full force once more, screaming, "Maaa!" over and over again.

"REE-tard! Stevie is a REE-tard!"

The front door was yanked open, scraping against its tight frame, and Stevie's mother looked out at us. Her face was thin, like a skeleton's, and she was wearing a thick housecoat. Grey and black hair floated around her head wildly. Beyond her, I knew were horrors too awful to imagine.

"Get away from here!" she yelled at us, shooing us with her left arm. Her eyes were round, fiery; she looked ready to kill us. We both answered with one more "REE-tard!" before running home. I had a stitch in my side and could barely run, but I was glad we'd taught Stevie a lesson about how things were supposed to be.

At Paul's house we slipped under his stairs and I felt my stomach sink. The road system we'd built was ruined, the dirt now gashed and mounded chaotically. I'd been holding my truck throughout the chase, and put it down tiredly. I felt hot and drained.

"Do you want to fix it?" Paul asked.

"No."

"Why?"

I didn't answer. We'd build it again, someday; I was sure of that. But Stevie could come back any time and destroy it, maybe steal our trucks while we were gone. We'd have to carry everything inside, protect it, if that was even possible. We'd never know what would happen to our work, or when.


But Stevie never did venture onto Goyer Street again. We saw him only a few times after that, when he would stand at the corner of Bedford and Wilderton watching us from a safe distance. As soon as anyone made a slight move in his direction he'd run away. We didn't bother to chase him. Half of me was afraid of what he might do; the other half was satisfied that we'd made everything right again.

A few days after we chased Stevie away, I came home from playing at Paul's a little before suppertime. My father's car was parked out front. But when I went upstairs I found no one around. I looked everywhere, then spotted my parents and sister standing on the back balcony. As I pushed the screen door open my mother turned and grabbed me, pulling me against her side.

"What's the matter?"

Other people were on their balconies, too, some pointing, some talking to each other, some even laughing. I looked beyond my mother's breast to the woods between Goyer's backyards and Barclay's, where I played almost every day. A car had somehow broken through the wooden fence behind the Barclay yard diagonally across from ours and rolled down the slope through the woods, to be stopped only by my tree. If my tree hadn't been there, the car might well have kept rolling all the way down into our yard.

I looked up, numb, at the car hanging crazily over our property, its light blue paint striped by late afternoon shadows, and its twisted chrome bumpers black in some places, glaring white in others. I saw a man standing by the hole in the fence, holding his chest, while some other people were talking to him or looking at the car. In the distance, I could hear a siren growing louder.

My sister sat on the iron steps of the fire escape, chin on palms, elbows on knees, staring at the scene. My father shook and scratched his head. "Incredible," he said at last, in a low, scary voice.

My mother just pulled me closer, but I didn't mind.

# The Book

*To Zaidy*

The first book I ever wrote was the one I did for my grandfather. I wanted to give him something to read while he was sick, so I wrote short compositions on the things that mattered— things teachers never asked you to write about—and comic pages featuring my spaceship, the Mars II. I wrote about our Sunday dinners, the black-and-white cat from next door that always ran when you approached it, and, above all, about my school. I told him about my successes at spelling, the kind of hymn book we used, and who the school bully was (Steven Thornton). He had his stroke just after school started. No one told me or my sister about it; we had to overhear my mother use the word when she talked to my cousin Ruth in the kitchen. At first I thought someone had rubbed him and he fell, and I didn't see why it was all being taken so seriously.

For a week after he had his stroke, my mother spent almost every afternoon at the hospital. She would fix lunch for us, but then we would all leave the house together, and she wouldn't be home when we returned from school. My sister was given a key—an honour I envied and resented mightily.

My grandparents lived in an apartment building on Bourret, across Côte Des Neiges Road which was, to me, the westernmost boundary of the known world. We sometimes visited them there, and I would savour the white brick exterior and the shiny lobby with its gold-specked floor tiles, all of which seemed luxurious. More often, my father drove over and picked them up, bringing them back to our place to share a regular or Chinese Sunday supper. Their arrival involved lots of noise and smiles as coats were taken to be hung up and Bubby and my mother exchanged the latest news.

"You remember Mrs. Acker, lives upstairs from me?"

My mother stood there thinking. "Yeah . . ."

"Crazy; her head is I don't know. Anyways, she fell on Tuesday."

"Fell?"

"Yeah, and broke her hip. Ambulance came and everything. Oy, she was never careful, her. Always running everywhere."

Zaidy was nearly bald by then, and whatever white or grey hair he still had stuck up and drifted as he moved. He shaved very closely, so that as he hugged me I could see his cheeks were red and streaked with little blue veins. He wore floppy shirts whose sleeves he held up with black garters just above his elbows. They looked so uncomfortable I wanted to see if I could wear them but he never offered to let me try them on. He always brought presents: usually a Superman comic for me and a barrette or something like that for Sheila. I hoped for more variety, but seeing the cover of the comic book, with its promise of colour and wonder, kept me from being too disappointed. I knew my birthday present would make up for it anyway.

The Sunday before his stroke Zaidy sat in the kitchen with my father talking about pensions. Pensions were part of the serious grownup world I cared nothing about—like *The News*, that boring first section of the Gazette, or the wasted half-hour of TV at six o'clock. I sat listening to them waiting for my turn, but never got the chance to tell him about the E (for Excellent) I got in spelling that week.

When we all sat down in the living room to watch Disney after supper, my father crossed his leg and rested a pad of graph paper on it, scribbling numbers under Zaidy's observation. Zaidy sat in the wooden chair he liked, backwards so he could rest his arms on the chair's high back. "Don't cash in the bond right away; it doesn't pay," my father said. "Keep it."

"No, sure." Zaidy seemed to know that so well it was almost insulting to remind him of it.

"But when it matures next year, cash it right away."

"Don't wait?"

"No. Right away."

Zaidy turned to me, a smile on his face.

"You hear that?" he said, pointing to me. "Right away!" I smiled back.

During a commercial I went into the kitchen to see what was going on. My grandmother was helping my mother scoop the remains of the Chinese food into one of the now-empty round cardboard boxes.

"She shouldn't have gone near him, you know," she said. "He was no good from the start. I didn't trust him right away. I mean, why would any boy. . . ? You know, she isn't . . ."

"I told her."

"I know you told her, but she doesn't listen."

"She never listens."

About a week after my grandfather's stroke, Ruth came to stay with us. She lived with Uncle Nat and Aunt Tillie, whom I never saw except at Bar Mitzvahs and weddings. Ruth was older than my mother, very tall, and stooped over, so that she looked more like someone out of a fairy tale than a relative.

She always wore striped dresses with buttonholes straining to hold onto the wide black buttons up and down the back.

While my father put the car away, Ruth lugged her huge brown suitcase up our duplex stairs; my mother tried to help her with it, but Ruth wouldn't let her. My mother directed her into the tiny room my father used as an office. Ruth swung the suitcase around my father's black filing cabinet and lay it across the cot my parents had rented for her. "So what did they say?" she asked.

My mother shook her head. "It's not good. Not good at all. His whole left side."

"Sugar." Ruth lowered herself slowly to half-lie, half-sit near the pillows. I didn't see how anyone that big would fit into so small a bed.

"He doesn't look the same at all, at all."

Ruth saw me standing outside the door. My father let me play in the office when he wasn't working in it, but now the room was entirely off-limits. "So how are you, honey?" she asked me. "How's school?"

"Okay."

"You do your homework all the time?"

"Of course," I said. What else did she expect? "Are you staying a long time?"

She shrugged. "How long it takes. Until your Zaida is well, eh?" She turned back to my mother. "Bella, are they going to keep him? I mean, they're not going to kick him out right away, are they?"

"No! He's in no condition." She puckered her lips. "We'll see him tomorrow."

After supper, we went into the living room to watch TV while Ruth unpacked, with Sheila's help. My mother looked through some papers she'd brought out of a bottom drawer of her bureau; they were kept in a black leather folder tied up with a thick string. Ruth came in later and dropped onto the chester-

field. She sat leaning toward the set, and I couldn't help looking at the curve of her back. I knew her posture would suffer if
she continued to sit like that, but of course I couldn't say anything.

"What's on?"

"*Lost in Space.*"

"Any good?"

"It's my favourite." It was my father's, too, or at least one
of them, and he sat with his hands behind his head, staring at
the set. But instead of concentrating on the show, Ruth kept
looking at the papers in my mother's hands.

"You should call Hi about that policy tomorrow."

"I was going to," my mother said. Did they have to talk
during the show? Couldn't they have waited till commercials?

"It's better if it comes slow, like. Not all of a sudden," my
mother said, then stopped herself. "I mean, I can't prepare. I
don't. . . ." She got up and went into her bedroom, and my
father rushed after her. Ruth sat for a while, then went back to
her own room.


From then on, my mother spent practically the whole day at
the hospital, while Ruth did the cooking and housework.
Normally, lunch was a bowl of Chef-Boy-Ar-Dee spaghetti
with cottage cheese in it, or a hunk of corned beef (the kind
that came in a tin you opened with a key) with ketchup, apple
sauce, and a banana. But the first lunchtime I came home, I
found that my plate had eggs on it. Not scrambled eggs, as I
had sometimes, but sunnyside up, with a slimy, yellow dome in
the middle. I'd seen this on TV before, but . . . I made a face
and asked: "What's this?"

"Eggs, of course."

I poked my fork into the yellow and the stuff oozed out.
Was she crazy? "They're raw!"

She laughed. "Don't be silly."

The white parts looked cooked, so I ate them and the Niblets she'd put on the side. And I had to ask her for the apple sauce and banana, as if she didn't know they were part of my lunch. I determined to tell my mother on her the first chance I got. After finishing the banana, I left the peel on the table and got up to go to my room.

"Hey!"

I looked up at her looming over me, pointing at the peel.

"What do we do with that, eh?"

"What?" She pressed her lips tightly together and waited, but I had no idea what she was talking about.

"Throw it out! Now!"

With all the exasperation I could display, I grabbed the peel and went to the garbage can, and I stepped on the lever as hard as I could. As soon as the top sprung up, I threw the peel into the paper bag bunched inside. Without looking at her I stomped past her to my room.

My sister came home then and I could hear her and Ruth in the kitchen. I hoped they would fight, but obviously Ruth had served her some cereal and bread-and-butter without mistake. At one o'clock, I put on my boots and coat and left without saying goodbye to Ruth, who was busy washing the dishes anyway. On my way to school I thought how good it would be for Zaidy to get better soon, so Ruth would go home and things would get back to normal. There were right ways and wrong ways to do things, and I wanted things done properly. But when my mother got home, and I tried to tell her what Ruth had done, she wouldn't listen to me. "You do whatever she tells you, Lawrence," she said. "Understand?"

Ruth was in the bathroom, which was next to the kitchen, and I wanted her to hear me. "Tell her to make lunch right. It's not fair."

"You're being silly."

I headed for my room to do my homework, but stopped at the kitchen doorway. "When is Zaidy going to be better?"

She looked up at me, her head resting on the fingertips of one hand. Her eyes were wider than I'd ever seen them, and there was nothing like a smile anywhere on her face. Instead of answering me, she shook her head slowly. I had no idea what she meant. Was she mad at me for asking? Was she telling me *No* to a question I hadn't asked? Or had she even heard me? I started to ask her *When?* but halfway through gave up and went to my room, almost resigned to the violation of our house's rules and routines.

Things didn't get any better. Ruth continued to do everything wrong: from when we had to do our homework (I missed many episodes of *Gilligan's Island* because of her) to what I had for breakfast (chocolate, not plain milk; what was Nestle's Quik for, anyhow?) to how we washed. I had to stand at the sink with my shirt off, and she scrubbed my arms so hard I felt my skin burn afterwards. And every mistake she made I pointed out to her, letting her know, "That's not what we do," or "That's not what I usually eat." Even my sister got upset when she wasn't brought on the Saturday trip to Steinberg's. Ruth did all the shopping herself, without Sheila's help, and naturally brought home Sugar Corn Puffs, which we never ate. We made her take it back.

My mother would come home from the hospital just in time for supper, and the first question my dad asked at the table was, "So, anything new?" Then he'd sit, twirling the curly hair on his head with his forefinger, while she talked about Zaidy.

"He couldn't eat at all today. They try to feed him but he won't touch it. Nothing. They don't want to put him on intravenous, but if he doesn't eat more they'll have to."

"Yeah."

Allan Weiss

"Oy, it's awful to see." She shook her head. But when she looked at me, she smiled, so I knew things weren't all that bad; Zaidy wouldn't stay so sick my mother would have to keep going to the hospital all the time. "One of the nurses is a real *chalaria*," she said to my father; "she doesn't wash him right. I saw her. She was so rough, like he was a piece of meat."

"Is Zaidy coming on Sunday?" I asked, pushing the boiled chicken through the sizeable puddle of ketchup I'd made on my plate. Anything to give it some flavour.

"No, honey," my mother said. Ruth sat silently (for a change) chewing on a piece of chicken breast she held with both hands. "He has to stay in the hospital some more."

"Can we go see him?"

"No, they don't let children up there. You can come to the hospital, though."

"Can I see him?"

"I said no. You can wait downstairs." She stared at me for a long time.

"Why not? I want to see him."

"You can't, Lar," my father said in his angry voice, which was actually quieter than his regular one. "Okay?"

"Why don't you make him a present?" my mother suggested. "I'll bring it up to him. He'll like that."

"Okay."

That would be good enough, for now. And I knew exactly what kind of present, too, or at least I did after rejecting the idea of giving him some of my trader hockey cards.


I spent the rest of that week working on the book, adding things to it even after I thought I'd finished it. If he could give me comic books, I'd give him some, too, and ones that were more action-packed even than Superman. My spaceship blasted aliens to pieces nonstop, zapping them with perfectly

30

straight rays that emerged from its guns and ended in blossoming explosions. Pieces of hull sailed off in all directions, thin lines showing their trajectories. Shots aimed at the Mars II were deflected by a squiggly force field surrounding the needle-nosed ship.

I wrote long passages of prose, too, about the highlights of my week in school. I told Zaidy about the assembly held in the gym where a policeman spoke (without an accent, despite his French name) about looking both ways and keeping clear of construction sites. I told him how boring it was to sit during Oral Reading listening to Garry Henderson struggle with easy words, while my eye travelled sentences beyond him. I wrote about my VG+ in spelling, and how I missed a word I really should have gotten. I described in detail the accident Zvi Rosen had in the schoolyard at recess when he tried to jump into a skipping-rope being rolled at pepper speed by Anna Schubert and Gail Moscovitch. Few boys ever bothered with skipping, but Zvi wanted to show that he was as good as any girl. Instead, he ended up ripping the knee of his pants.

It was all there, complete, in words and pictures—things that had really happened, things I'd made up. For the compositions I had used sheets from my mother's letter-writing pad, which wasn't really paper but something called Vellum, and for the comics I used the backs of order forms my dad brought home from work. After my dad stapled the pages together (at the top, because I'd neglected to put in side-margins) I was surprised at how thick the book was, and very pleased because it was so full.

On Sunday, we all drove to the hospital, squeezing into the car and bumping down side-streets to Côte Ste. Catherine. We parked behind the hospital and walked around to the main entrance. I'd never seen a building so big; it seemed to be one huge mountain of brown bricks and windows. We walked without speaking down the curving sidewalk to the glass doors, and into the lobby where dark metal and upholstered chairs stood in rows before a flower shop and a circular desk that said Information. Ruth, Sheila, and I sat down to wait—Sheila with a book of various puzzles, me with a book of connect-the-dots—as my parents took the elevator upstairs, my mother carrying the book in her purse. It pained me that I wouldn't get to see the look on Zaidy's face when he saw and opened it.

The others in the lobby were mostly old people. Taxis would pull up outside the door and the drivers—often dark-haired little men with cigarettes in their mouths—would come in to help an old lady or someone with luggage out the doors and into the cab. Beside us, an old man sat in a black overcoat, hands forming a single fist around the top of his cane. He was muttering something and swaying forward, as if he were *davening*. It reminded me of the time Zaidy took me to the Young Israel for a Sunday Service (that was the only morning he didn't work at the store where he swept up and carried crates of fruit). I watched the men *daven*, and Zaidy held the prayer book in his hands. I could follow some of the words, but the rabbi said the prayers so fast I got hopelessly lost. When I looked over at Zaidy's book to see what page we were on I noticed he was holding it upside down. He wasn't even looking at it, but was muttering the words with his eyes focused on the back of the seats in front. I laughed quietly at the joke, and pulled at the book to turn it around. He just glared down at me, no smile on his face or in his eyes, and I let go. "Shhh!" he said sharply, and I felt like crying.

It seemed like hours—and hundreds of puzzles—before my parents returned and sat down beside us. My mother's expression was very serious, and she didn't say anything. My Dad sat beside her and stroked her forearm. Ruth then pushed herself up and walked slowly, arched forward, to the elevators. Finally, we were alone.

"Did you give him the book, Mommy?"

She looked down at me and smiled weakly. "Hm? Yes, dear. He liked it a lot. It was very nice, a very nice present." Then she looked out the front doors, and didn't say anything until Ruth returned. All she said then was, "Let's go."

Later that week, I overheard my mother say that they'd moved Zaidy to another hospital, the Hospital of Hope. I figured that meant he was getting better, but nobody would tell me anything. I asked Sheila but she didn't know any more than I did. And Ruth kept on doing everything wrong, even after we told her how to do it right, and I saw how hopeless she was. She was like all the substitute teachers I'd ever had; they would have us do French first thing in the morning rather than just after recess, or forget the Lord's Prayer, until we complained and corrected them.


One night I was awakened by the ringing of our phone. I knew it was very late—much too late for phone calls—so I got out of bed and went to my door, which I kept open to let in light from the hall's chandelier. My mother came out of her bedroom wearing her long pale blue nightgown, knit slippers, and the strange hairnet I saw very rarely. She picked up the phone after its third ring and said in a sleep-scratchy voice, "Hello?" She listened for a few seconds, then her hand went up over her mouth and nose; she said nothing at first, and what I could see of her face seemed angry. Meanwhile, my father had come to the bedroom door and was motioning at her questioningly with his head, his eyes narrow and his gold print pyjamas awry. "Thank you," my mother said strangely, then put the phone down and ran to the bedroom, disappearing into it with my father. It was the first time I'd ever heard my mother cry.

Now Ruth was standing in her doorway, and when Ruth saw me she gestured for me to get back to my room. But in spite of her I stood there watching. I could feel my eyes sting

Allan Weiss

from sleepiness and the bright chandelier, but I blinked a lot to keep them open. My sister was now up and looking on from behind me, swinging the door between her thumb and middle finger. Ruth came, and without a word closed the door on us. I managed to get it open again in time to see my mother and father come out of their room again, this time almost fully dressed, except that neither wore stockings.

"They said I should come right away," my mother told Ruth. Ruth pointed at me, and my mother gave me a look so horrible I rushed back to my bed without hearing anything she might have said to me.

I fell back asleep quickly, and slept for what seemed like an incredibly long time. I knew something funny was going on when I woke up without anyone calling my name. I went into the kitchen and found Ruth sitting there drinking almost white coffee out of the green mug she used. She looked up at me as I came in, nothing readable in her eyes. I looked up at the clock: 9:45!

"Hey! I . . ."

"You're not going to school today. Your mommy and dad had to go out."

An unexpected holiday was always a special one—like when a blizzard cancelled school. I glanced out the window to see if the weather had anything to do with this, but saw nothing wrong. "Why?" I asked. I sat down at the kitchen table and waited for her to get my chocolate milk and bagel, which she did very slowly.

"They'll tell you when they come home."

My sister got up later and slumped down across the table from me looking as if she hadn't slept at all. But she ate her Alpha-Bits at normal speed, barely allowing them to be moistened by the milk before she scooped them up with her big spoon.

"We're not going to school," I told her.

"I know. How come?"

I shrugged. After breakfast I got dressed and went into the living room, where I turned on the TV. Ruth immediately rushed in and punched it off, almost jamming the switch right through the set. "You can't watch TV," she said, interfering as ever. That ruined the "holiday," of course, but I went into my room and spent the morning re-organizing my hockey cards into keeps and traders.

Strangely, I don't really remember my mother telling me about Zaidy, although I remember not crying at first because I didn't think she was telling the truth. Not that she was lying, but I figured she'd gotten things mixed up. I did cry later, but not because of what she told me in the weird language she used ("passed away," "out of pain," "no more suffering"). I cried because she was sad, and my father was sad, and my sister was sad; being sad was all I could be, and Zaidy was still in the hospital, and Ruth would continue ruining our lives for who knew how long.

My mother sat with Bubby in the kitchen that evening. I heard my mother say, "It should be just just." I knew what she meant, but could not have explained it to anybody. She repeated the sentence to my father later on: "It should be just just."

"I know."

"You hear me? The shiva will be here; Bubby can't . . . she can't." She held her mouth tightly, then through her fingers said, "Just just."

That day Ruth did something very strange, and it convinced me even further that she didn't know what she was doing. She went around washing the mirrors using something called Bon Ami, but instead of cleaning them she just smudged them up so badly you couldn't see yourself except in the very low parts, where she couldn't reach or see very well. I decided that if my parents didn't say anything, neither would I; after all, the mirrors were theirs. But the mirrors were left that way.

After the funeral everyone came back to our house, and I became lost in a crowd of strangers. I recognized only Uncle Nat, Aunt Tillie, and Aunt Ellen, my boring great-aunt who spoke no English; she just sat at one corner of the couch smiling at everyone who nodded at her. Two old people who my mother said were my zaidy and bubby from Chicago were also there, but I stayed away from them; they weren't my real grandparents.

People brought trays of food: crustless mini-sandwiches filled with salmon and other, unidentifiable, horrible-tasting things; a dish of kugel; some bagels from Van Horne Bagel Bakery sliced and heaped with cream cheese and butter; danish of various gooey kinds; and spice and honey cakes. Ruth had gone to the funeral, too; we'd been left with Mrs. Archambault, our landlady. She did nothing that whole morning but watch TV. She was careful to turn it off as soon as the family came home, and left without saying goodbye to us.

Till now, I'd been certain how to act; the atmosphere in our home left little room for confusion. But everyone sat around talking, joking, laughing, as if this were a party. Uncle Nat was a loud talker—I remembered him from a Bar Mitzvah we'd gone to a year before—and he didn't try to keep his voice down. He had shiny black hair slicked back from his forehead, and sat hunched forward, challenging everything anybody said to him.

"Pearson's a better man than Diefenbaker ever was!" he told one of my uncles, whose name I didn't catch. "Diefenbaker was all talk. Pearson'll stand up to the Communists."

Kitchen and folding chairs (borrowed from Mrs. Archambault and various relatives) circled the living room. There were also two low, dark wooden chairs near the entrance to the room; my mother and grandmother were the only ones who sat in them, and they never sat anywhere else. The chairs were just the right size for children, and I wondered why

Bubby and my mother always chose those small hard chairs to sit in. Both wore black dresses, and black neckerchiefs tied on the side. As uncles, aunts, and cousins came in they went to Bubby and my mother and held their hands while saying how sorry they were. Bubby cried a little, but my mother didn't cry at all then, although she looked as if she might.

I knew I'd seen these people before, and recognized their names, but to me they were just huge adult bodies filling our home. And Ruth towered over all of them, carrying trays and offering coffee or Eskimo Ginger Ale. I was introduced to people I'd met at the Bar Mitzvah, but vaguely remembered: Aunt Sophie with her sweaty smell, Uncle Moishe who drove down from Ottawa for the funeral, Uncle Sam with the thin moustache.

While Bubby was in the kitchen doing something I went over to where my mother was and sat down on Bubby's chair so I could talk to her, to ask her if I could go outside. But before I could say anything she half-shrieked, "Don't sit there!" I jumped up. "Oy, don't ever sit there, Lawrence. Why would you want to sit there?" She rubbed her forehead with her hand. What had I done?

"Those are special chairs," she said more calmly.

"Why?"

"Never mind," she said, not looking at me. "Just please don't sit on them. Go play in your room," she told me, and I went, angry at the lack of explanation.


By supper most were gone, and Ruth and Bubby were the only ones who stayed to eat Ruth's leftover brisket with us. But after supper many of them returned, along with people of varying ages who hadn't been there that afternoon, and a man with a short grey beard who, I was told, was a rabbi. There were babies, and some girl cousins Sheila's age who disappeared with her into my father's office, but I had no one to play with except Ruth's brother, David. I took him to my room and showed him my comic-book collection.

"Wow!" He flipped through them. "They're all Supermans." The look on his face confirmed what I already knew: that I had a pretty valuable collection, almost a whole set. "Where'd you get them all?"

"Zaidy gave them to me."

"Oh."

Which reminded me . . . I left him still going through the comic books, and went out to the living room, half-tiptoeing to where my mother was sitting. She was talking to Uncle Louis, the one with the bulging stomach. "Mommy, where's the book I gave Zaidy?"

"What, dear?" Her eyes were so strange—as if she didn't really know I was there. "I'm not sure. Ruth took everything home from the hospital." She smiled tiredly at me. "Don't worry; it's not lost. Anyway, it's time for the *Kaddish*, so please be quiet for now, okay?"

My father, who had spent most of the day in arguments with my uncles, came by and put his hands on my shoulders, steering me towards my room. "Don't make trouble," he whispered, looking serious. David had been standing in my bedroom doorway waiting for me, but now came out and stood with my uncles. Uncle Moishe passed around a small basket filled with black yarmulkes. The men stood facing the same way, while the rabbi held a small black book in his hands, and *davened* as he and Uncle Sam recited some Hebrew words; my father, David, my cousin Henry, and my other uncles stood silently behind them.

I found Ruth sitting on her cot in my father's office, putting some *True Confessions* magazines into her suitcase. "What is it, honey?" she asked.

"Did you see the book I made Zaidy?"

"Yeah, just a sec." She took her big black purse from my father's desk and dug through it. "Your Zaida didn't have much there. Here." She pulled out the thick wad of paper; the cover—a blank piece of paper on which I'd drawn a picture of the Mars II—was hanging by only one staple. "I'm sure he liked the pictures. It's kind of a funny present to give him, though."

"What do you mean, funny?" I asked, taking it from her and checking for missing pages. She'd really wrecked it.

"Well, you know, honey, your Zaida couldn't read."

I balled my fist and hit her as hard as I could on the shoulder, again and again, gritting my teeth as I swung, while she stood up and turned away. "Hey!" she screamed, over and over. "Are you crazy?" When she turned away, I hit her below a button, wanting to break her bent back. My father ran in and got hold of me. He dragged me out, and we ran right into my mother.

"Is it so much to ask?" she yelled, tears rolling out of the corners of her eyes. "What's the matter with you?" My aunts and uncles tried to stay out of it, except Uncle Nat, who was saying something like, "He's only a boy, he doesn't understand." I tried to get out of my father's grip but he wouldn't let go. The look on my mother's face was an agonizing mixture of sadness and anger, and I almost hated her then for making me feel so bad. She waved at me dismissively and went to sit on her chair again, while my father brought me to my room. "To be just just," I heard her say behind me.

"What's going on with you?" he demanded as he shut the door on us. "You gone crazy or something?"

I sat on my bed, holding the book tightly in my left hand. "She said he couldn't read."

"Who? Oh." He didn't say anything for a while. "You should ask your mother about that. And tell her you're sorry. Ruth, too. Don't move." I sat waiting triumphantly. I would finally get to tell my mother on Ruth once and for all. She came and stood before me, arms folded in front of her, while my father leaned against the door jamb.

"She said Zaidy couldn't read."

My mother looked at me hard then, eyes on mine—seemingly for the first time in ages. "He was embarrassed. He didn't want you to know."

"But he bought me books."

"He knew those were for children."

"Say you're sorry," my father said. I had no idea what to apologize for, and I wouldn't do it anyway. Not to her, and especially not to Ruth.

But she just put her hand on my shoulder and gave me a weak smile. "Never mind," she said. "Try to stay quiet, okay?"

I nodded. I didn't know why she wasn't going to make me apologize, but I was relieved. They left to go back to the living room, where everybody was talking to each other again.

Ruth finally went home the next day, pulling her giant suitcase down the stairs. I watched her from my room, holding my bedroom door slightly open so I could see only enough of her. At last our house was right again, and the only thing I allowed myself to feel was satisfaction as I watched the hall door close on her.

# All the Birds That Fly

When I was young I knew that God existed. I'd been told about Him for as long as I could remember: by my parents, and then by TV, and finally by school. He was really there, and you could feel Him when the wind blew, hear Him when there was thunder, and almost see Him when a widening ray of light broke through a hole in the clouds, just like on the cover of *The Child's Book of Bible Stories* in our classroom library. He watched my every move, and I could picture Him staring at me from inside my head, beyond deception or excuses.

I also knew what He wanted from me, or at least I thought I did. He wanted everyone to pray to Him, to show we knew He was there, and to ask Him for what we wanted. From kindergarten on, our class at Bedford School said the Lord's Prayer every morning, right after singing *God Save the Queen* and *O Canada*: we would bow our heads, and pronounce the strange words (as well as we could) in unison. Sometimes as I said the prayer I became afraid of being punished for trespassing into people's backyards when I went exploring, especially in the woods beyond the fences lining my neighbours' lawns. I even invented my own prayer, which I said (or rather thought) every night—not kneeling in a nightshirt beside the bed, hands pressed together like the old-fashioned boys in the readers, but lying in my bed staring up at the ceiling and aiming my silent words to Heaven. I asked God to bless my family and friends, and help me do things the way he wanted, the proper way. We sang hymns, too:

> *Who made ocean, earth, and sky?*
> *God, our loving Father;*
> *Who made all the birds that fly?*
> *God, our loving Father.*

That hymn always reminded me of the dead sparrow I once found in the woods beyond my own fence. I'd squatted over it and poked at it with a stick, examining its dark grey parts: the head's empty eye-sockets and open beak, the skinny legs, the feathers on its bent wings fluttering in the wind. Those were the things God used to make His birds so they could fly almost as high as He was, when they were alive.

Bedford was in the Protestant School Board of Greater Montréal, and my teachers were mostly Gentile. While they didn't talk much about Jesus we did essentially Christian things, especially at Christmas. But it didn't bother me that while other kids were getting loads of presents, I received only Hanukah gelt, which was one real silver dollar from my grandmother and a mesh bag of chocolate coins in gold foil from my parents. Getting masses of gorgeously wrapped presents was a non-Jewish matter and therefore had nothing to do with me. On the other hand Santa Claus was part of my world because he was everywhere, and I enjoyed making his face in Art out of construction paper and cotton, which my mother gladly supplied. In fact, my Santa Claus was one of three chosen to be displayed on Parent-Teacher Night, and I was thrilled. "It's very nice," my mother told me, smiling proudly, as she cupped my chin from behind.

The hymns, of course, were Christian, too. Most of the kids in our class were Jewish but we stood there and sang things like *Onward, Christian Soldiers* and *Jesus Loves Me, This I Know* anyway. We liked Christmas carols better, because they were prettier, although the line in *The First Nöel* about Jesus being the King of Israel confused me terribly. But I didn't really think about what I was doing; I sang the hymns and carols because I was supposed to—everyone was supposed to—so doing anything else was unthinkable.

In Grade Three, my parents enrolled me in Hebrew School. They weren't very religious people; they almost never went to shul and never spoke Hebrew, although my mother did speak Yiddish, mostly to her friends or my grandmother. But they wanted me to prepare for my Bar Mitzvah, and for my mother, at least, it was very important that I learn about the traditions. "You should know the traditions," she'd say, "even if you aren't a real religious." She meant the people I sometimes saw on Bernard Avenue in black hats and long black coats, the men with beards and the kids with *paiuses* hanging in coils by their ears.

At Hebrew School Rabbi Steiner taught us to read Hebrew, and while we didn't actually learn many words, we could read whole passages of Hebrew as long as the vowels were printed. We had to know how to read Hebrew script to be able to recite *brochahs*, even if we didn't entirely know what those blessings meant. He also taught us to celebrate the Jewish holidays—at Hanukah he gave out small plastic *dreidels* that we spun at our desks and trapped before they curled their way over the edge— and explained the origins of each one, describing in detail the horrors our ancestors had suffered at the hands of Gentiles centuries ago. Rabbi Steiner made it very clear that the Jews had been persecuted for centuries, that we had survived because God had protected us, and that we finally found safety when He gave us back Israel. Rabbi Steiner was usually pretty boring, but when he talked about how much God had done for us he almost started yelling. He was small, except for his big belly which made his tie bend to the right, but in spite of his size he could talk with so much energy it was scary. I'd look up from my orange-covered notebook only long enough to be sure he wasn't yelling at me specifically.

"We knew we were the chosen people! And so no matter what Pharaoh or the others did to us, whatever suffering they put us through, we had faith. God was with us, and we knew He'd save us; He'd always be there! In ancient times, in Germany, in 1948, when the Arabs tried to massacre us, too, God was looking out for His people!"

I saw God as a giant lowering His hand to keep the arrows from crowds of Jews huddling in the desert, or killing our enemies by simply willing them dead. He watched over us and took vengeance on our behalf. We had nothing to fear because no matter what was done to us, we would triumph in the end.

The more I learned at Hebrew School the more worried I became about what I was doing at regular school. We were different; our holidays were not their holidays; our language was not their language; yet almost every day I sang to their Lord Jesus. I did so only because I was told to, and I hoped God understood that. When I sang *Silent Night* or *Hark, the Herald Angels Sing*, I did it mechanically, keeping my voice low while reminding myself—and therefore God, who could hear everything I thought—that I didn't and wouldn't ever believe what I sang. One day, after having said the Lord's Prayer every day for years, I decided to pay careful attention to the words, to make sure there was no hidden reference to Jesus in it. I was very relieved to find none.

I also began to think back with horror on something that had happened the previous summer. I was going to Neighbourhood House Day Camp. Most of the kids in the camp were Jewish, and so was Mr. Horowitz, our counsellor, but we went on a field trip to a church. We piled into the yellow school bus and drove through mysterious parts of Montréal until we arrived at the tall stone towers. A real nun—looking like the kind we saw on TV and in books—came out of the church and smiled down at us, head cocked. You couldn't see any of her hair; with her black cowl she looked bald and weird.

"You will come inside, uh?" she asked us in a French accent. We followed her into the church through one towering open door. The church was a lot like a shul, but darker, and with higher ceilings. Facing us at the opposite end was a huge statue of Jesus. We all walked slowly down the aisle, and Jesus got bigger and bigger, hanging from his cross over the gold-sparkling altar. Stained-glass windows on either side made a rainbow of his white skin, and candles flickered in countless long rows along one side of the altar. The size of Jesus, of the church, and all that colour and light made me want to fly like the birds, rise up . . . I looked at the nun who was telling us when the church was built and by what order. She smiled down at me and I smiled back, deciding that even though nuns were strange they were nice, too, and so were their churches—in fact, I wanted to come back some day.

Now, though, as I thought back on that field trip I pictured God watching me walking down the church aisle, frowning his displeasure at my betrayal. I was sure He'd been horrified by my thinking I'd like to go back to a church, even if it would be just to look; I hoped my ache of guilt would make him forgive me.

I also began to wonder about my parents. They were Jewish but they didn't go to shul every Saturday the way Rabbi

Steiner said Jews should. One evening after Hebrew School, while my mother was clipping Steinberg's coupons out of the Gazette, I knelt on one of the kitchen chairs and asked her why we never went to shul.

"We go," she insisted. "On the High Holidays. Not all the time," she admitted, "but that's only the Orthodox."

I knew what Orthodox meant, and it sounded right to me. "Aren't we supposed to, though?"

"Who says we're supposed to?" She ran the tip of the scissors lightly down the newspaper page, stopping when she found a coupon she could use, and carefully cut along the dotted line.

"I thought we just are. Jews are supposed to celebrate *shabbos*."

She smiled. "Do you want to get up early every Saturday morning, put on a suit and tie, and sit listening to a rabbi all morning?"

I thought about it. "No. Not really." Saturdays I could sleep in and watch cartoons.

"Neither does your father." She put the coupon aside and looked at me. "You don't have to belong to a shul to be a good Jew."

"Okay." But I still wasn't satisfied, and as I went into my room to do my homework I thought that when I had my own family, I'd definitely take them to shul, even if it meant getting up early on Saturdays; that was so far into the future I didn't worry about it too much, anyway.

But one way or another I'd let God know that I knew what He wanted from me, and that I was on His side.

My chance came at the end of Grade Three, when my parents registered me for sleeping camp for the first time. My mother asked me whether I'd rather go to Camp B'nai Brith or Green

Acres, the two camps near each other in the Laurentians. I thought the choice was obvious. Although some of my friends were going to Green Acres, I wanted to go to the camp that sounded more Jewish, where I'd probably learn how to be a good Jew. I was nervous about going, but my parents and friends kept telling me how much fun camp was. I wasn't all that anxious to go to a place that sounded so much like school: having to get up early, grown-ups telling you what to do every minute. But this would be more like Hebrew School, where I'd be doing the right kinds of things all day, maybe even playing Jewish games.

My mother got out my grandfather's old black trunk from the garage locker and packed it following the camp's mimeographed checklist. As they suggested, she ordered cloth labels printed with my name and spent an entire Friday afternoon sewing them into my clothes. It was strange seeing my name in block letters on all my T-shirts and underpants. She packed a can of "Off" and a small bottle of pink liquid she said I should use for mosquito bites. She bought me a hefty supply of comic books at Woolworth's, including many about heroes I didn't know. Then, on Sunday morning, my father put my suitcase in the car trunk and we drove to Coronation School where my bus would be. As he drove, my father kept glancing up at the dark clouds starting to build overhead.

The schoolyard was crowded with kids and parents. Suitcases were piled everywhere. A row of tables with hand-lettered signs for the different camps stood near the yellow buses lined up in the parking lot. I noticed many boys wearing yarmulkes, and I thought with panic that we'd all be expected to have one. But nobody said anything as I got into line in front of the small table marked Camp B'nai Brith where an old lady sat checking off names on a sheet of paper.

My parents and Sheila stayed with me right up to the check-off, while a huge man in a short jacket took my suitcase and added it to the mound growing beside one of the school-buses.

"I gave you plenty of paper and envelopes and stamps," my mother said. "You'll write often?"

"Yeah."

"Okay, campers only after this point," said a man who was walking back and forth behind the tables.

My mother grabbed my face in both hands and kissed me. I cringed. One kid somewhere near the buses was crying, but I vowed not to do that, and anyway I didn't feel at all homesick.

"Have a good time," my mother said. I could tell she was just about ready to cry, too.

"Yeah," my father said. "I expect lots of letters."

"Sheila?" my mother said. My sister wasn't at all sure what to do or say, so she made a comical face and gave a fast wave. I waved back.

I had to join another line up to get onto the bus, and when I was properly in place I turned, but couldn't see my parents anywhere. As I looked around at the other kids I only saw one boy I recognized: he'd been in my Grade One class but I couldn't remember his name. I tried to catch his eye but got no response, and I wasn't even sure he was really going to the same camp or whether I'd see him there if he was. I didn't know how things worked.

"All aboard, guys," the man in the short jacket said in a heavy French accent, and we filed into the bus, some of the boys running to grab specific seats. I sat in the first empty seat I found and pressed up against the window. I didn't know how long the ride would be and I was sorry that my comic books were in my trunk and not with me. Another taller boy sat next to me and I looked up at him. He gave me only a glance, then turned to talk to someone he knew across the aisle.

By now the noise in the bus was deafening, the way it was on field trips at day camp or school. The bus finally lurched into motion, and as it turned out of the schoolyard I saw a crowd of parents waving madly, some of them craning their necks to see if they could find their kids inside. If my parents were among them, I couldn't see them. The bus turned up Victoria and headed into parts of Montréal I'd never been to before: houses, apartment buildings, streets—all unfamiliar and all seeming to go on forever. We eventually crossed a bridge, and soon we were on a highway going through total wilderness like the kind we drove through on our trips to the United States. Someone on the bus started up *Old Hiram's Goat* but I didn't feel like singing.

Suddenly the bus was lashed with rain falling like silver spears, pounding on the top of the bus. The sky was still pretty light—summer storms never seemed as dark as fall or spring ones—but the rain was so heavy the windows of the bus were coated with water. The bus' windshield wipers pendulumed furiously to keep up, but as soon as they cleared a space, rain filled up again. I began to wonder where I was going, and why. For the first time I felt a pang of homesickness, but swallowed it.

The bus turned off the highway onto a gravel road and we crunched along under a canopy of arching trees that filtered the rain a little. We rode through the darkest forest I'd ever seen (darker than anything in New York State or Vermont) until we made another turn and emerged into a clearing. A tall arching sign read Camp B'nai Brith in wooden letters. The bus pulled up outside a large house that wasn't at all a log cabin—it could have come out of my own neighbourhood. Some people in slick black ponchos came out of it as our bags were unloaded onto the muddy ground, and we were led off the bus. Everything outside was dripping and the smell of pine was overwhelming.

"What's your name?" one of the men in ponchos asked me, shouting above the rain and holding a clipboard he tried to protect with his hand.

"Lawrence Teitel."

"Teitel, you're in Bunk Number 9. See that building over there? No, no, up that hill! Yeah, pick out your bag and bring it up there!"

I found the old trunk among the other suitcases and lugged it up the muddy hill, up a gravel path that made the trip at least a little cleaner. It led right up to a barn-like wooden building with "9" carved into a plank over the door. I pulled open the screen door and found myself looking into what might have been the barracks from *Gomer Pyle*. Half the beds, or rather cots, were already taken, as boys—all strangers—sat on them or were jamming their suitcases under them. I picked an empty one and stood the huge trunk at its foot, then sat down on the scratchy blanket, watching the rest of the bunk fill up with kids I didn't know. Some of them seemed to know each other, though, and began to talk, while the rest of us sat alone, waiting.

The bunk was huge, and I counted eight cots on each side. The wall at the back had what I took to be a back door, but no windows. I looked for signs this was a Jewish camp—Stars of David, Hebrew words, menorahs—but the walls were just bare planks. I went to my suitcase and swung it up onto the bed, then rummaged through the clothes which had shifted out of their neat piles, until I found my comic books. I flicked through them, not knowing what was supposed to happen next.

The rain had almost stopped; outside, just a few drops pattered against the ground. I looked out through the screen door. The sun was breaking through, and the trees in the distance were lit up against a still dark sky. A man in a poncho with the hood lowered came up to the bunk and pulled the squeaky screen door open. All eyes turned to him.

"Hello, guys," he said. He had longish hair and a beard, and I wondered what a beatnik was doing here. "My name is David and I'm your counsellor. If you have any problems, see me." He pulled off his poncho. Underneath he had on a lumberjack shirt and jeans. "Settle down! HEY! Now, this is your schedule: wake-up is at 8:00; we go down to the Mess for breakfast . . ."

He hung the poncho up and I tried to absorb the fact that I had to get up at the same time as I did for school.

". . . everyone in the Bath House for showers; at 11:00 is Morning Swim Class for those who can't float; noon is lunch; from 1:00 to 3:00 is Rest Period—that means you stay in the bunk. Is that understood? You're not allowed to go out without permission. 3:00 is Afternoon Swim Class for everyone." He stopped and stood with his hands on his hips. "HEY! After Swim Class we have Field Activities, then supper, then you write letters home, then activities: Mondays is Science, Tuesdays and Thursdays Arts and Crafts, Wednesdays Jewish History, and Fridays and Saturday morning we have *shabbos*. Saturday night is Special Events. Is that understood?"

It was. I realized with a shock that even he wasn't wearing a yarmulke; I thought at least the officials here would be Orthodox.

"Fine. Wait here until suppertime, then." He walked to what I'd thought was the back door, but it turned out to be the door to his room. He went inside and closed the door behind him; soon the sound of *I Wanna Hold Your Hand* came through it.

I lay down and read my comic books slowly so that I wouldn't go through them all right away. There'd been a rule about not bringing toys, but I didn't see why since there was nothing else to do here. The boys who knew each other talked—mostly shouted, actually—among themselves; the rest of us didn't want to cross the lines marking off the spaces around our bunks.

But then a boy in thick glasses, with a knit yarmulke bobby-pinned to his hair, came over and looked at my stack of comic books. "Are all those yours?" he asked, incredulous.

"Yeah. Why?"

"Do you collect them?"

"No. Kind of."

"Can I read one? I don't have any. I won't rip it or anything, I swear."

"Sure," I shrugged, and gave him an *Incredible Hulk*; I didn't much like Marvel Comics, anyway.

"I didn't know we wouldn't have nothing to do."

"Me neither."

He looked at the masking-tape label my mother had stuck to my trunk; it was already peeling off because of the rain. "Your name is Lawrence?"

"Yeah," I said warily. I was afraid he was going to make fun of it.

"Are you Jewish?"

"Of course I'm Jewish!" Why else would I be at B'nai Brith?

"Some aren't, you know. My name's Chaim. That means *life*."

"I know." I'd studied that much Hebrew. "Are you Israeli?" I'd always wanted to meet a real Israeli.

"No. Thanks."

He took my comic book over to his bunk and began reading, and I tried to pass the time till supper.

That evening David led us to the Mess Hall, which was a flat, rectangular building down the hill. It faced onto the round clearing where the bus had left us, and in the middle of the clearing was a flagpole with no flag on it. In the Hall the whole camp sat around huge round tables organized by bunk, although the counsellors ate somewhere else. We were served by waitresses in green uniforms and hairnets. I didn't eat much because I didn't like the stuffing they gave with the tiny piece of chicken, and the scoop of mashed potato they put beside the chicken was dry. We got Jello for dessert (in fact, that was the only dessert we ever had) and nothing else: no chance to get more chicken, no snacks for later. Then we were walked back to the bunk to stay until bedtime, when we had to change into our pyjamas in the same room as everyone else. I crawled under the sheets of my bed to do it. At 9:30 came Lights Out, and David left the bunk, saying: "Not a word, guys, do you hear? Get some shut-eye." I lay staring out the screen door at the tall lamps scattered throughout the camp grounds. A mosquito whined in my ear but I couldn't catch it; a moth fluttered against the screen door, trying to get out. I said my made-up prayer, certain that God would be satisfied with where I was. The homesickness came back, but I held it in; two of the other kids, though, started crying.

The next morning David woke us up and brought us down to the Mess Hall for breakfast. But before going in we were made to stand in the clearing; at the top of the flagpole was the Israeli flag, and an older man came out of the two-storey house. He waved his hands to silence us, but didn't succeed completely.

I was standing between Chaim and a boy from my bunk named Joel, who was part of the group of kids who knew each other. I asked Joel, "Who's he?"

"He's the Camp Director, dummy. Mr. Alter."

When we were mostly silent Mr. Alter said to us: "For those of you who are new to B'nai Brith, welcome. We start every day by honouring our homeland." He began singing the *Hatikvah*; I only knew the first line or so, but followed the rest. Chaim knew all the words, and I thought how great it must be to know everything you needed to know so well.

I found out that first day that we were expected to spend most of the time inside our bunk. That's what Rest Period was:

we were supposed to find something to keep ourselves busy between lunch and Afternoon Swim, although my mother had sent me to camp to get some fresh air. We didn't see much of David, either, except when he led us down to the Mess Hall or the lake. I couldn't swim, so while David played with the boys who could a woman counsellor tried to get me to learn how to float.

"Just let go," she said as she helped lower me backwards into the water. "Don't bend your back like that; close your eyes and let go." I wanted to do it, but it wouldn't work. For some reason I couldn't relax, or understand what she wanted me to do. I looked up at the clouds sliding across the sky. I knew God was up there, and I half-seriously asked Him for help but he didn't make me float, even as the cold water crept up to my ears and beyond. The water covered my face and I burst free, coughing and spitting out the water. "Come on," she said, "try again."

I also couldn't learn to shower with the other kids. I was shocked to see the Bath House, with its single room and nozzles sticking out of the wall. "Come on! Chicken?" the others said, but I wouldn't do it, and no one could make me. My mother had taught me what was proper and what wasn't, and this wasn't. David suggested that I could at least wear my bathing suit, but I wouldn't even go that far. I wanted to go home, and I told my parents that in my first letter.

What most disturbed me about the camp, though, was that apart from singing the Israeli national anthem in the morning and Wednesday night History, there was very little that was Jewish about it. Our Field Activities were regular games like the ones we played at Field Days at school: dodge ball, races, baseball games. In the evenings we learned how to make silhouettes out of leather, and clay medallions and ash trays. My comic book supply ran low, but I learned to my relief that there was a library in the back of the Crafts Hall. But most of the books were in English and were about space or dinosaurs, or novels like the ones in my classroom library. There were some books about the Bible, but none that didn't seem very familiar.

On Wednesday, the camp rabbi, Rabbi Spelman, talked about the sorts of things I usually only learned at Hebrew school. We sat in the Assembly Building on hard wooden chairs, some paying attention, others giggling in the back rows, as Rabbi Spelman explained about Passover and the Ten Commandments. To my relief, yarmulkes were supplied: plain white ones kept folded and piled in a straw basket at the door, to be returned at the end of the lesson.

I knew most of what Rabbi Spelman was saying, but it was refreshing to do something fully Jewish for a change. Altogether I wasn't learning nearly as much as I'd expected; I didn't think I'd ever be as devout as the boys on Bernard Avenue, or even know as much as Chaim—who was becoming my friend—but I wanted to be as Jewish as possible.

Then on Friday night we had a *shabbos* meal, with soup, challah, and candles on the tables. Yarmulkes were passed around, and Rabbi Spelman led us in the *brochahs* as the candles were lit by some of the waitresses. Mimeographed sheets with the blessings in Hebrew and English transliteration had been placed beside our plates, but I tried to ignore the English letters and read the Hebrew as quickly as I could:

"*Baruch atoh adonai elohaynu melech ha'olam, asher kidishanu b'mitzvotov v'tzivanu, l'hadleek nair shel shabat.*"

I watched Chaim, who said the service almost entirely by heart, the way the old men in the shul did. I dreamed of knowing Hebrew, as well as the lessons themselves *that* well, but knew I'd never reach the point where I could read Hebrew

55

without the vowels printed underneath the letters. I was embarrassed by how little I knew, and angry at my parents for not teaching me more.

After dinner we went to the Assembly Hall, where Rabbi Spelman held the service. My grandfather had taken me to a service once and I'd started to cry for no reason. It might have been because of the voice of the cantor as he sang what seemed unbearably sad songs (even though I couldn't understand the words), or how serious everyone was. This time I could sit calmly through the service, but it still made me feel sad.

After the service Rabbi Spelman sat down on a chair in the front row. Mr. Alter stood up to talk to us.

"Boys, it's very important that you all remember your Jewish heritage, which is more than just being from a Jewish family and going to shul every Saturday. It means knowing God and having God in your heart always. Do you all keep God in your heart always?" Most of us said, "Yes, Mr. Alter." "Good," he continued, "because these days what with all the crazy things going on—the rioting, the rock music, all of that—it's sometimes easy to lose your way. Am I right?"

Obviously he was.

"But God is always there for us. Even when you disobey His law or the laws of the country you're in—Canada, or Israel—He'll never abandon you, as long as you don't abandon Him. If you believe in Him, He'll always be there for you. Is there anyone here who doesn't believe in God?"

To my amazement, a boy on the far side of the room put up his hand, and some kids giggled. I stared, utterly shocked, at the raised hand.

"Can you stand up?" Mr. Alter said.

The boy stood.

"You really don't believe in God?"

"No."

"I'm sure He believes in you, eh?"

We laughed. "Tell me, if there's no God, who made you?"

"Well . . . my parents."

Of course . . . but he was missing the point. I rooted for Mr. Alter.

"And who created them?"

"Their parents."

"And the first parents?"

"It's all evolution."

"From monkeys. We come from monkeys, is that it?"

The boy wouldn't quit. "Yeah. Kind of."

"*Kind of.* Tell me, who made the monkeys? Who made the whole Earth?"

"I don't know."

There! Everyone laughed, and I laughed, too. We'd found someone who didn't believe in God, and shown him. And as I laughed I felt good inside because I knew God was listening; I knew he'd hear me laughing and see whose side I was on. He couldn't be in any doubt any more. After the boy sat down, Mr. Alter, who'd laughed, too, said, "Okay, everyone, you can go back to your bunks, now."

I left the Hall happy, feeling light as the wind, but knowing I couldn't explain why to anybody. I wanted to look up and say, "Okay?" but didn't dare. My point was made, anyhow; there'd never be any doubt again.

# Minorities

Montréal is a city of minorities. It's the major city in Québec, home of the French-Canadian minority in Canada. It's where most of the English-Canadian minority in Québec lives. And within the English minority is the Jewish one that I once belonged to. So everybody was part of some minority, but being in that position made us proud rather than frightened; it was sort of like those contests in which people brag about the hardships they suffered, trying to top—or maybe bottom—each other.

In any case, each group was so tightly knit that no one seemed to feel all that vulnerable. We could always count on each other, while they (whoever "they" happened to be at the time) were threats only as far as we let them be. At hockey games the P.A. announcer called out the goals and penalties in French and English, which was, to us, perfectly normal; just as normal was the fact that we enjoyed seeing English players do well, showing the French that we, too, knew how to play the game. They would never defeat us completely if we could produce Ted Harris and Dick Duff. And as Jews we had to compete with the English Christians as well, although by the time I was going to school the McGill quotas were gone, and we no longer worried about who the Pope was and whether he was "good for the Jews." I remember my grandmother asking that about Pope Paul VI: "Is he good for the Jews?"—and my father just gave her a quizzical stare.

Normally, Jewish kids went to schools in the Protestant School Board of Greater Montréal—a title that seemed gloriously impressive. I didn't know what the Protestants were protesting against, but I knew they were Christians and therefore irrelevant. Most of our teachers were Christian (except for Miss Eisenberg who became Mrs. Finklestein), but most of the students at Bedford School were Jewish, as far as I could tell. Thus, we had nothing to worry about. They never had us sufficiently outnumbered to be a real problem.

On the other hand, there was one French-Canadian kid in my grade, Denis Bourgeon. On the first day of class Miss Shaw called out his name and pronounced it "Dennis," and he made it a point to correct her. "De-nee," he said, in a challenging voice that characterized him immediately as a troublemaker. Miss Shaw looked up through her glasses with their sharp-cornered turquoise frames and said: "Day-nee Burjohn."

"Present."

Then she made that mysterious but important-looking mark in her attendance book. Teachers never made more than a tiny symbol, and I never actually got to see what the symbol looked like, but knew that the less the pen moved the better. Those marks were part of the teachers' world, like their lounge on the first floor, and it was almost comforting to know that they had these little mysteries they shared only with each other. Clearly, they knew what they were doing. "Rhonda Burak?"

"Present."

I took a few moments from that anxious time of waiting for my name to be called to look at De-nee. He was taller than most, with a face that looked like it had a permanent sneer. He came from that other side, that strange world we sort of lived in but never really knew. As he sat there, hands folded like the rest of us, I found myself wanting to see just a little of what he'd seen. The only French kids I'd ever met were the ones my friends and I chased down Wilderton because they spat at us, when I was four years old.

Actually, Denis didn't seem particularly foreign. I could recall no bizarre accent disturbing the harmony when we'd all stood up to say the Lord's Prayer. I wondered what he was doing in our school, rather than in a Catholic one. "Lawrence Teitel?"

I picked up my hand and said, "Present," waited for her to make her mark and turn her attention elsewhere, then looked at Denis again. He looked back at me, probably wondering what I wanted, then tried to ignore me. I had to concentrate on Miss Shaw from then on because she was passing around the hand-written mimeographed list of necessary supplies: two HB pencils, geometry set, ruler, eraser (pencil/ink), Canadiana coloured pencils; the usual stuff, as if all the teachers had gotten together on their lists, too. Miss Shaw handed out our textbooks, which we had to put into paper book covers showing the history of the alphabet. As I struggled to fold them as per the instructions, tucking the covers of my geography book into badly formed sleeves, I glanced over to see if Denis knew of some esoteric technique for doing this. But he was also having trouble. Only the girls ever got the folds right.

First days were always half-days, so at noon we all went home, savouring the last freedom we'd know for eternity. Howard Cohen and I headed for our houses beyond Darlington, while Denis walked in the opposite direction, toward the apartment buildings near Côte Des Neiges. "You going to get the stuff now?" Howard asked.

"I have to give my mother the list, dummy," I told him.

Howard was even shrimpier than I was, and it was fun pointing out the obvious to him. He seemed to like being pushed
around. "We'll probably go to Stan's or something." Stan's was
the best variety store in the neighbourhood: it was crowded
with school supplies, chocolate bars, caps for our guns (when
we were little kids, of course), and sports cards for every season. Stan himself was a fat, bald man who never smiled, and
served us only when all the adults in the store had paid. We
always vowed to get even with him for that, but never did.

"We're going to go to Woolworth's."

"So?"

"It's cheaper."

Howard's family was in dire poverty; I knew because he
was always talking about the cost of things and how much he
couldn't afford. I got ten cents almost every day for two packs
of hockey or baseball or football cards, and had a pretty sizeable collection by now. It was unthinkable for my mother to
run out of dimes. But Howard never had any allowance, and I
considered him utterly pathetic. His father didn't work, for
some reason.

"I have to go now. Bye," I said, and ran up the stairs of my
duplex to present the list to my mother.

Denis proved to be more trouble than I'd expected. It wasn't
just that he'd talk whenever Miss Shaw left the room. He and
Gordy Paschik invariably began whispering back there as soon
as Miss Shaw was gone, and their voices rose progressively
until they were loud enough to be heard all over the school.
She'd come back and say something like: "All right, who was
talking? Come on, speak up! All right, if you won't confess I'll
keep everybody in after school until you do." Neither Denis
nor Gordy would confess, so we'd all have to stay in. I could-
n't understand why I was being punished for something some-

one else was doing. I always did what was expected of me; I never spoke, and I always sat facing front with my hands folded, meeting my part of the bargain. So while I was getting pretty impatient with Denis, I learned to hate Miss Shaw.

But even beyond that there was Oral Reading. We'd be asked to read out passages from our books, and Miss Shaw almost always asked the worst readers rather than the best. I would breeze through my three or four sentences, interrupted only by her cries for "Expression!" "Use more expression," she'd say, and I'd modulate my voice, raising and lowering the pitch to produce something other than a monotone, although I know I overdid it. Janet Zimmerman was also a good reader, and between the two of us we could have gotten the whole class through Oral Reading in record time. But Miss Shaw insisted on calling on Denis, and Gordy, and Peter Kostos; I'd sit there straining under the frustration as they sounded out the words, my eyes racing to the end of the paragraph, then having to trudge back to where the reader was. I'd rest my cheek against one hand, then the other, looking up as the second hand on the clock inched its way around the numbers.

". . . and . . . the . . . foree . . ."

"Foreign."

". . . foreign . . . con . . . countries . . ."

Why not let them do this after class, when the rest of us were at home? I ran my finger along the edge of the pages, feeling the smoothness disrupted by the slightest upward movement.

" . . . trad . . . traded . . . other . . . goods . . ."

For furs! Was it so hard? The words glowed for me, opened themselves to my eyes. How could anyone not see them? And while Denis had very little accent he had trouble with words like "the" and "then," which came out sounding as if they were spelled with a "d." I watched Miss Shaw watch Denis or Peter, hating her for making me sit through their struggles.

I would find myself getting exasperated with Denis as his reading dragged on. But at least he had hockey cards. I generally traded only with a select group—Howard, Wayne Fischman, Bobby Sklar, and Jeffrey Gold—flicking through my deck while they announced whether they were interested. "Have. Have. Have. Need. Have." Normally everybody had at least three of some barely recognizable player like Ron Schock, but nobody could get Gump Worsley. The best way to obtain cards, actually, was to toss them against a wall—closest takes all. Denis and his friends played that every recess, and he wasn't bad at it. He used the two-finger spring technique (hold the card at the edges, bend it, and let fly), one I could never master. I preferred the motion we'd later use for Frisbees.

The funny thing was that I never heard him speak French to anyone. We'd started to learn French in Grade Three, but that meant nothing more than another set of routine fill-in-the-blanks. *La porte, le chat*, scattered words like that. And French was what you heard flipping around the TV dial, seeing bizarre dubbed versions of American shows like *Bonanza*. On *Chez Hélène*, Suzy the Mouse learned a few words and phrases from Hélène, but little more. For some reason I wanted to hear whole sentences from him, accent and all. It seemed wonderfully weird that someone could spend his whole life talking that way, without ever using English.

One recess I walked over to where he was playing and took up a position near the champ squares to watch the action. Gary Ingham landed one with a corner touching the wall; Denis sailed his high and scored with a leaner, the bottom of which sat triumphantly on Gary's card. I nodded in approval. He went over to pick up his prize and saw me standing there.

"What d'you want?"

"Nothing."

He went back to the line and prepared to fire again. Gary was clearly getting upset; he'd lost the last three rounds. Denis won easily. He looked down at one of his new cards and made a face at it. "Hey, you pick up my cards I'll give this to you."

"What?" I looked at the card he offered: Jean Béliveau! "Sure!"

"I got three now, eh?" He killed Gary over the next four rounds, and I scooped up Denis' winnings and brought them over. I was certain I'd never actually get the card—no one would give up a Jean Béliveau just like that—but sure enough as soon as the bell rang he handed over the card and smiled, apparently glad to find someone willing to work so cheap.

"Thanks!"

"Yeah." We lined up to go back in. I added the card to my pack and jammed the whole thing into my jacket pocket, fully aware of who got the better of the deal.

I was careful not to look at the card during class because Miss Shaw had confiscated Gary Littman's collection earlier that week for paying more attention to it than to her. Jean Béliveau was my favourite player and I'd been looking for his card all year. At lunchtime I took it out and stared at it before leaving my seat. All the cards that year showed the player's picture superimposed against a colourful painting of a section of rink and stands, with a Toronto Maple Leaf, of all things, skating off to the right. Each had a rectangular silver and woodgrain border representing the screen of a television set. Béliveau's name (without the accent) was in poorly-printed yellow beneath his picture. It still smelled of sugary bubble gum.

I put the card on top of my pile, not caring if it was out of numerical order, and walked home achingly proud of my acquisition. If Denis wanted me to do the same work again—for, say, Bobby Hull—I'd jump at the chance. I wanted to show the card off to my friends, but part of me wanted to keep them out of this, at least for now. When I got home I told my mother about it, as she spooned my cottage cheese into a bowl, and even got the card to show her.

"Who gave it to you?"

"Denis. This guy in my class."

"A Fransoyce?" That's how she pronounced it. She looked at me in surprise. "That was nice of him," she said half-heartedly. Her next line was supposed to be: "Did you say thank you?" That's what she always said in these circumstances but instead she took my banana down from on top of the fridge, checked it for colour, and put it on the table beside my cottage cheese. As I peeled it, pulling off all the little strings that could make you gag, I imagined the collection of superstars I could collect for virtually nothing.

My mother didn't say anything to me the rest of the lunch hour; when my sister came in and began heating up her Chef-Boy-Ar-Dee spaghetti, my mother asked her a few questions about school, then went to watch *Search for Tomorrow* at 12:30.

"I saw your stupid friend Gary again after school," Sheila said to me.

"He's not stupid."

"He keeps calling me names. Tell him to quit it."

"I did. It doesn't help."

"Well, tell him again." She spun her fork around in the spaghetti, which was swimming in pale red sauce. "I heard Miss Shaw's strict."

"Yeah. She isn't fair, either." I thought about how she acted when someone talked and began to wonder why I should bother staying quiet.

"I had Mrs. Lester in Grade Four. She was nice."

"Miss Shaw makes you do things in front of the class." It was true; if you didn't do your homework she put your desk at the front of the class so everyone could see you write out some sentence twenty times. Paul Wasserman didn't comb his hair one morning and she combed it for him in front of everybody. We laughed at him, of course. And she tried to correct David

Purich's posture by making him walk while she pushed his spine straight, but he couldn't keep it that way. In fact, in later years he bent over more and more. I never found out why.

When I described some of that to Sheila she said: "God! I'm glad I didn't have her."

After lunch I went into my room and got my pile of cards out of my jacket pocket. At the back was my checklist, and I pencilled in the little square box beside Jean Béliveau's name.


From then on Denis and I were sort-of friends. Howard and Jeffrey Gold were still my best friends, but Denis and I often met at recess and lunch hour to trade cards. I asked him about where he lived and what it was like living there, but he just shrugged and told me an apartment, as if that explained anything. I could never imagine living in one; I pictured a tiny box with virtually no room to move in, and no access to a huge back yard like the one I had. But I'd seen and heard enough to know French-Canadians were poor, and probably used to conditions like that because they never knew anything better.

I also asked him why he'd given me such a valuable card that day, and he told me: "I got a thousand cards, eh?"

"No, you don't!"

"Yes, I do."

A thousand cards . . . that was more than anyone could possibly save. A thousand cards would mean stacks of them filling a room, piled everywhere. He just shrugged at my skepticism and described his collection, insisting that he would have more but delivering *La Presse* didn't earn him enough money.

"Can I see them?"

"Sure. Some time, eh?"

Back in class, Miss Shaw went around to all the desks looking inside to see how we were keeping them. She had rules about having your books in proper order: the big geography book at the bottom, history book on top of that, and so on until the speller. On the other side were supposed to be our exercise books, pens, rulers, and other items from that list. My desk was usually pretty messy, and so was Jeffrey's. Miss Shaw turned Jeffrey's desk over, spilling the contents around his feet. His eyes widened and his mouth tightened. While we watched he knelt and tried to get his desk back in order. I didn't know whether to find the scene funny or not, but I imagined what I'd do to her if she tried that with me.

"I want your desks kept neat!" she yelled suddenly, addressing the whole class but keeping her eyes on Gary who was under my desk retrieving a stray pencil. "I won't have a mess!"

I looked at her, standing there beside her large desk, hand on the blotter. I'd always done everything right: I'd never missed doing my homework, or played hooky, or talked when ordered not to. But I saw that that didn't matter, that if she wanted to she could turn my desk over, too, without warning. There were no rules for her.


About a week after Denis gave me Béliveau he invited me to go over to his house to see his collection. He lived at the other end of Goyer, in one of the almost identical brown apartment buildings that lined both sides of the street from Wilderton to Côte Des Neiges. I passed about ten of them every day but had never been in any of them, although I'd gone into the alleys behind them a few times. Denis stopped outside his building and I looked up, both scared and thrilled by it. We entered a narrow area between two glass doors, and I looked over the buzzers and mailboxes while he found his keys. I'd never been given a set of keys and figured he must be older than the rest of us, that he must have failed a grade or two.

Inside, the hall smelled of cabbage. I watched an old lady in a housecoat and slippers trudge up some stairs to the lobby carrying a laundry basket full of puffed-out clothes. She glanced at us, then disappeared down the hallway to the right. Denis twirled his finger next to his ear and led me upstairs. The halls were painted blue over rough plaster, and the banisters were glossy black. We stopped at a brown door with a brass '6' nailed to it; through the door came the sound of a TV. Denis unlocked the door and pushed it open.

*"Maman? Vous êtes là?"* he called, with a thick accent that sounded terrifically exotic.

We went into a small foyer between the kitchen and living room. The TV was tuned to a French interview show, but nobody was watching it. The living room was full of plants: under the window blinds, all around the walls, on the rectangular coffee and end tables. As I'd noticed at other friends' houses, the apartment had a strange smell to it.

Denis shook his head. "She left it on again," he said. "She has to take a lot of naps, you know."

"Oh. Is she sick?"

"Yeah. Blood something." He tried to find the right words for it but gave up after a few seconds. He went in and closed the TV; at that moment a door opened down the hall beyond the kitchen and a woman came out trying to smile through that angry look you get when you just wake up. I'd seen my mother look that way often when she came to wake me up. Denis' mother was pulling a sparkly brown robe around her, and squinting through narrow-rimmed glasses.

*"C't'un ami,"* Denis told her.

She nodded. "Hello." She walked slowly down the hall, her pompom-tufted slippers pattering on the carpet, and disappeared through another entrance into the kitchen. "What's your name?" So I told her. "You're hungry?" she asked, still hidden by the kitchen wall.

Allan Weiss

*"Non,"* Denis answered for both of us, then tapped my arm to follow him down the hall. As we passed his parents' room I saw the unmade double bed and beside it a stand crowded with pictures, including one I thought was of a policeman. But before I could make it out he'd led me beyond the doorway and into his room. I looked around, marvelling at how much stuff he had. The top of his bureau was jammed with models: Superman breaking through a brick wall, the Robot from *Lost in Space*, the submarine from *Voyage to the Bottom of the Sea*. Viewmaster reels were scattered over the bureau and a small white desk was cluttered with exercise books, hockey cards, and comic books. We took our jackets off and threw them onto the bed, under which I could see two baseball mitts, and a hockey set beyond them. Scotch-taped to the walls were small portraits of Indian chiefs—the kind I'd seen advertised on the back of a cereal box: Pontiac, Geronimo, Tecumseh . . . he clearly had the whole set.

He reached under the bureau (pushing aside a plastic army helmet) and pulled out two shoeboxes stuffed with cards. "These're just the hockey ones, eh?" We sat on the floor and I tried holding the cards as he piled them into my hands. He really did have hundreds, and as I checked the numbers on the backs I saw he was only missing a few. He had cards I'd been searching for but was never able to get, like Gump Worsley and the Canadiens team picture.

And I realized how hopeless it would be to try to get any of them. He'd never trade with me because I couldn't offer him anything he didn't have. Naturally, I couldn't ask him to just give me any. But at least they were there in my hands to be looked at, and I knew I'd never forget seeing them. I'd hoped he'd show me wonders, and he did.

His mother appeared in the doorway, looking a little more awake and brushing her long black hair behind her ears with her hands. "Everything okay, Lawrence?" she asked. I nodded.

"I don't feel so good, you know," she continued, and I noticed how strong her accent was. "I get tired easy."

"Come on," Denis said, reaching under his bureau again and bringing out still more shoeboxes. He had baseball cards, football cards (both American and Canadian), cards from TV shows like *Combat* and *The Munsters*. All his collections were in fantastic shape, and he had some full sets. His mother watched us for a little while, then left. Later, when I was leaving to go home for supper, I saw that her bedroom door was closed, and the TV was on again.

My mother was busy stirring some boiling potatoes when I got home. She asked me where I'd been and I told her about Denis' collection. I half-expected her to feel guilty that she couldn't give me enough allowance to build up that kind of collection, but instead of talking about that she asked: "So he's a nice boy?"

"Yeah."

"Good," she said, as if pleasantly surprised at the news.

"Why?"

"So many of them are anti-Semites." She sat down opposite me and rested her cheek against her hand. "When I was a girl they used to follow us, call us names, me and your cousin Ruth. They'd come in a gang." I sat there trying to picture the scene, relishing it for all its horror. Gangs! What she was describing belonged to a world I found both incredible and compelling, like reading the Classic Comics version of *Oliver Twist*. "*Maudit juif,*" they'd say, and maybe come after us. But your Uncle Hi and Uncle Nat would get their friends and scare them away." She smiled. "Back then your Uncle Nat was tough, all right. You didn't fool around with him."

"He's still pretty tough." He had the harshest voice I'd ever heard, and he scared me whenever he came over. Once I overheard him telling my other uncles that the Russians and Americans would never go to war. "The next war is going to be

71

between the White race and the Yellow race," he insisted, and the others nodded or shrugged.

"Well," my mother said, "I'm glad your friend doesn't call names."

At supper, when my father heard about Denis he said: "You have a Pepsi in your class? Is he a Moroccan Jew or something?"

"I don't know." I knew Catholics had all kinds of crosses and religious pictures in their houses, but I hadn't seen any of that at Denis' place—just the usual sorts of decorations: calendars, paintings of country roads, photos.

"Whatever," he said, mashing up the potatoes on his plate with his fork.

I knew from Hebrew School that the Catholics had long hated us, that the Pope had said nothing while Hitler was killing six million of us, that they blamed us for killing Jesus. In fact, before going to Denis' I'd half-hoped that I'd see some Catholic stuff there, which I imagined would be weird and lurid, and maybe even dangerous in some way.

At recess I asked Denis a lot of questions, and he answered them readily at first, then began to say things like: "Why d'you ask?" I really wanted to know about his family, although I didn't know how to ask about what was wrong with his mother. So I asked about his father.

"He's not home much, eh? He's in the army doing special stuff. I don't know."

"Where's he go?"

"All over. Why?" I shrugged. "My mother, she's always sleeping so sometimes I have to make my own supper. I hate that." I almost said "Wow" but kept quiet. "Look at this." He opened his schoolbag and showed me a postcard-sized black-and-white picture of Henri Richard. "I sent away and got it in the mail today. Neat, eh?" It was. Looking closer, I saw that Richard had autographed it! "It's the best, eh?" Denis said, shaking his head. "I got to show this to Gordy. He won't believe it." And he went off to find Gordy Paschik, leaving me standing there agonized with envy—not just of his autograph, either; his life was full of real hardships, of the kind found only in our readers or in comic books: a sick mother, a father who was never home, maybe priests brainwashing him with sensational lies—it was like a Saturday afternoon science fiction movie, with all its delicious horror.

I went inside and walked quickly to my classroom, hung my coat up on its usual hook out in the hall, and headed for my desk. Howard Cohen was standing by my desk waiting for me and before I sat down he asked, "Are you still my best friend?"

"Sure."

"'Kay." I hadn't played with him in the schoolyard for quite a while, spending most of my time watching Denis play cards, and saw him only occasionally after school. He returned slowly to his desk, and sat there running his pencil over and over a line he'd drawn on the cover of his exercise book.

Denis was showing the autographed picture to Peter Kostos, in full view and risking its seizure. But he didn't seem at all worried, and when Miss Shaw came in the picture disappeared—into his desk or pocket—so that everything was, on the surface at least, just the way she liked it.

I didn't want to lose Howard as my best friend, but Denis' poverty was more interesting (after all, Howard did live in a duplex), and his problems were more serious, more important. His world fascinated me, while Howard's just depressed me.

Denis continued to have trouble with Oral Reading, so of course Miss Shaw kept calling on him. He'd struggle through a sentence, and almost give up when he had to pronounce a word containing "th." With most of us, Miss Shaw would just ask for more expression, and we'd modulate our voices accordingly. Or she'd make the worse students sound out the words, giving impatient sighs whenever someone came up to a word for the second time and still couldn't get it. But with Denis it was always the same problem, and Miss Shaw would shake her head. "This is English, De-nee. Th." I ran my pencil around the inkwell in the desk, wishing I could send the "th" sound by thoughtwaves to his mind and out his mouth.

At last Miss Shaw got tired of him, and motioned to him to come to the front of the class. "Stand here and repeat after me," she said, adjusting her glasses and staring hard at him.

"The."

"De."

"The."

"De."

"Come on!" Her voice rose to the pitch that told us she was getting mad. It was the voice she used when she told us we had to stay after school, when she'd told Angela Boratto to stand in the corner for letting her history book fall to the floor with a bang that made everybody jump. "You're not trying! Try! The."

"De." Denis's mouth tightened, and he blinked rapidly. Part of me wanted to stand up and tell her to shut up, but another part wanted to watch, horrified and fascinated all at the same time.

"Stop wasting my time. This is an English class and you're going to speak English properly! The!"

"De."

Some kids laughed, even one or two of those who sat in the back with him. What would it be like to stand up there, the whole class watching you, the teacher mad? I'd been brought up to obey teachers, and accept that they could do nothing wrong, that what they did was what they were supposed to do.

I couldn't accept that any more, but I didn't know how to stop her, and I wasn't sure I wanted to, at least right away.

I thought Denis would start crying, but he didn't. He just stood there, listening to the laughs, to Miss Shaw keep on saying, "The," except that he'd stopped saying anything. After what must have been her tenth try he finally said: "I can't."

"Go back and sit down," she ordered him, and he walked by my desk, face hard as stone.

"What are you smiling at?" he asked me. I didn't even know I was smiling, and didn't know what to reply. He kept going, and I turned to watch him sit down. He sat staring at the desk, breathing deeply, while the room got very quiet.


We stopped being friends after that. He kept on playing cards with Gordy and a couple of the other kids from the back of the class. I once invited him over to my house to see my comic book collection but he said he had to get supper ready for himself and his mother, and I never asked him again. But after school he'd walk in the opposite direction down Goyer Street, and I'd imagine following, to see what would happen.

# October

I've always found October to be a strange month to have my birthday. As a kid I thought birthdays belonged on sunny, summer days, but the days leading up to my birthday parties—with their candles, brightly wrapped presents, and crêpe-paper hats—were cold and windy. I would sit in the kitchen ready to blow out the candles on my cake (one extra for good luck), beneath cheery, shimmering blue and white streamers Scotch-taped to the walls, while outside the trees stood stripped to their skeletons. October was the month of early darkness and thick gray clouds, and especially Hallowe'en.

I anticipated Hallowe'en almost as much as I did my birthday; in fact, cutting jack-o'-lanterns out of orange construction paper and helping decorate our classroom windows with black cardboard witches seemed much more appropriate for the season than cake covered with rosettes and my name in blue icing across the top. From my school readers I associated October with owls and scarecrows, ravens and straw, blackened farm landscapes, full moons against starless night skies . . . Birthdays were for summertime; for October, Hallowe'en was right. And we kids considered it our holiday, even more than Hanukah—another time of collecting presents as if they were our due.

So October was my favourite month almost as much because of Hallowe'en as my birthday. In fact, even as I unwrapped my presents—the G.I. Joe equipment, the Aurora model kit of the Batmobile or a TV spaceship, the inevitable article of clothing from my grandmother—I would look out the window at the grey, autumn dusk and wonder what costume to wear that year.

Near our school was a house that made Hallowe'en particularly vivid for me and some of my friends. It was a real haunted house, meaning that it looked like a haunted house and clearly no one lived there. It was a grey clapboard, two-storey house with many corners that stuck out at strange angles (unlike our perfectly square duplexes). The steeped roof and the gables over the protruding windows were all black. Out front was a sordid-looking porch over which hung black, sloping planks supported by unpainted wood beams, and in the yard stood a dead tree.

At recess one day Paul Wasserman and Zvi Rosen swore they'd seen ghost lights moving in the upper window as they were walking home from after-school soccer the night before; we all made fun of them, but partly believed them, too.

"You're lying," I said to Zvi. I didn't know him very well, because this was the first year we'd ever been in the same class, but his story was too good to be true.

"I am not," he replied in a definite voice. I wanted him to be telling the truth, so I accepted his word and shrugged. I remembered all the times I'd seen him do things no other kid I knew would do, like jumping into the girls' rope-skipping routines just to show off, or running across Bedford without looking. If anyone would be likely to meet ghosts, it would be him.

"What did they look like?"

Paul didn't say anything, so Zvi answered, "Like lights, moving." He sneered. "So, don't believe me! I don't care."

That clinched it; it had to be true. The bell rang and we went back inside, but I found it hard to get Zvi's words out of my mind.


On the Saturday after my tenth birthday I met Zvi at Woolworth's, where my mother had taken me to buy my costume. We always got a costume one size bigger than the box suggested so that it would fit over a winter jacket. But there weren't many choices left in my size. I selected a Pirate; the Devil looked too cheerful and the growing number of super-heroes—Batman, Superman, Green Hornet—seemed irrelevant. Hallowe'en wasn't a time for good guys; it was the one holiday that allowed us to indulge our love of gore and shock, encouraged rather than stifled by our parents. Going out as The Hulk or a Prince missed the whole point.

"Hey, Lawrence!" Zvi came over from where his mother was sitting, balanced unsteadily on one of the lunch-counter stools and drinking a cup of coffee. She was the fattest mother I knew. My own mother was rummaging through a pile of socks on a table marked "Clearance."

"Hi. What're you going as?"

"I don't know." He flicked through a couple of boxes. They always put the mask on top because the thin cloth underneath, folded at least a dozen times, told you nothing about the costume. "I don't even know if I'm going this year."

"I'm going to be a Pirate this time."

"Oh, yeah?" He fingered the bottom of a Superman box. I could see that the zipper on his jacket was torn from the cloth.

My mother would never let me walk around like that; she kept buying me new and uncomfortable clothes. The worst time was the first day of school; every year she made me wear new oxfords that were so stiff they scraped the skin off the backs of my heels. Whenever we went out shopping she always embarrassed me by straightening this and untangling that. Today I'd had to wear the new, scratchy pants that my grandmother had gotten me for my birthday. My mother always encouraged her to buy boring things: "He gets enough toys," she'd say. "Get him something he needs." I understood that Bubby might not know what toys to get, but my mother insisted that she buy gifts I could use rather than play with. "So you shouldn't look like a shlump," my mother explained.

I pulled a Dracula from the steel rod on which the boxes hung and said, "Here, this is better."

"Okay." He ran to his mother with the box and showed it to her. She nodded and returned to her coffee.

We all left Woolworth's together, my mother and Mrs. Rosen walking side-by-side so they could talk. Zvi's mother looked much better when her large front was hidden under her huge grey overcoat. She talked with a thick Israeli accent, and an image came into my mind of desert nomads, sandstorms, people almost dying of thirst . . . I wondered, briefly, why she was here when my Hebrew School teacher had always said all Jews would end up back home in Palestine.

"On Hallowe'en you're supposed to play tricks on people if they don't give you junk," Zvi said.

"No, you're not."

He gave me a look of disbelief. I felt stupid and hated him for it. "Of course you are! Why do you think you say, 'Trick or Treat'?"

It hadn't occurred to me because no one had ever refused. The door would open and a stranger, or a friend's mother, would grab a handful of candy from a bowl in the hall and deposit the load into our paper shopping bags. Some would drop pennies into our UNICEF boxes as well. But no one faced us and said "No."

"What do you do?"

He shrugged; he'd never had to play a trick either. "Too bad I don't live near the haunted house. That'd be great on Hallowe'en, eh?"

I nodded. Not just great—perfect.

"Hey!" Zvi yelled. "Let's go."

"Where?"

"Come on."

I tried telling my mother where I was going, but she was too busy talking to Mrs. Rosen to notice me. We ran down Wilderton in the stiff wind, the leafless trees around us shaking their naked branches at us. I barely kept my footing going down that steep slope. We passed the wide, grassy plateau I'd once explored and found depressingly boring, and the white-brick duplexes whose brilliant elegance my Lego bricks could never reproduce; we crossed Wilderton and I stopped, winded, my chest aching in the cold air.

"Come on!" Zvi called when he saw me lagging.

"Wait up! Where are we going?"

"The haunted house, dummy."

"Now?" It was broad daylight—not a time for scary things. But he was the expert on the house, and it made sense to follow his lead. It was almost four o'clock, so the sun was already pretty low in the sky.

"You chicken?"

"No." If he'd said "scared" I might have said yes, since that was the whole point of the haunted house. "But don't you have to tell your mother?"

He looked at me as if I were a big baby. "Of course not. I never do."

It had never occurred to me to ignore my mother. She usually worked so hard to make everything safe, and proper, and telling her where I was going seemed a natural part of all that. I found the whole idea of not caring what your mother knew or thought shocking but thrilling, and I envied him.

We mostly walked, and sometimes ran, the rest of the way to Bedford School, approaching it from Bedford Road. The school looked strange from this angle (I usually entered from the Goyer side), especially without the classroom lights on. Its windows were covered with our Hallowe'en creations and the decorations the teachers had put up: witches on broomsticks, bats, hissing black cats. We ran past, to the field not far from the railway tracks that led downtown.

The house stood in the middle of the field, completely separate from the apartment buildings and duplexes around it, as if trying to keep its distance. Beyond the pointed roof, clouds raced by in the wind, but the dead tree was almost motionless. A picket fence, its wood grey and unpainted, bordered the field, but it was too low to be a real barrier. We walked around the outside of the fence first, crouching like soldiers in a war movie and looking, half-fearfully, half-hopefully, for movement inside. To my surprise all the windows looked pretty normal, except for the basement windows which were boarded up.

"Shhh!" Zvi hissed for no apparent reason, though it seemed right. He motioned me to follow, as he kept low, eyes fixed on the house. "I saw the lights up there." He pointed to an upstairs window. I looked at it as long as I dared, then averted my eyes. If something should . . . Zvi now squatted with his back to the fence, his eyes on mine and full of suspicion. He was sure I'd run away, but I wouldn't give him that satisfaction. "You ready?"

"Yeah." My knees were in the mud that barely held the fence up straight, and my oxfords were spotted with patches of quickly drying dirt. Now I looked right for the part, an adventurer soiled by his exotic travels. It was like when I walked to school after a heavy rain; I'd stick my shoes in the ooze that formed in the parking lot of the car wash near Darlington, looking for quicksand.

We stood up, still crouching slightly, and swiftly pulled ourselves over the fence. My foot almost got stuck between two pickets, and I had visions of being trapped there, unable to escape the horrors that awaited us in the house. But I pulled my foot free in time and landed not far from Zvi.

"Come on!" he whispered, waving his arm like a company commander. We ran to the house, heads lowered, as if no one—not even a ghost—would be able to see us run across the open field. Soon we were on the dank porch itself, on planks of rotting wood aiming long splinters at us. Zvi stood pressed against the grey wall, beside the narrow front window; chips of the cracked paint snowed onto the porch. I was nearer the door, back against a ridge of molding. Zvi motioned that he would look in the window while I was to look through the door's glass plate. He counted off three seconds with his fingers, then pointed at me.

Through the door I could see a hallway leading to a flight of stairs. A brown carpet covered the floor and the centre of the staircase. Above the hallway was a black chandelier full of small frosted bulbs that were all still unbroken. Nowhere did I detect cobwebs or layers of grey dust, or black shapes flying or skittering by. I tried opening the door, but it was locked. I turned to signal Zvi to that effect, but he was gone.

My chest seized. I looked back across the clearing to the fence we'd scaled and saw no one, not even the back of someone disappearing into the woods. And I couldn't see him making his escape in any other direction, either. For a second it crossed my mind that the house had swallowed him somehow.

"Come on!"

Zvi's head was sticking through the window—from the inside. Before I could ask him how he'd gotten in I saw that the window frame was so rotten he'd been able to jimmy the window up and now had to hold it to prevent it from crashing down onto his neck. The wind he was letting in sent the curtains on the other side billowing madly, a sight which in itself was enough to make me hesitate. I wanted to say, "Are you crazy?" but I knew he'd just call me chicken. Anyway, I thought of what I'd be able to tell the guys later, and how they'd admire me for actually going into the haunted house. And how they'd make fun of me if I did chicken out. While Zvi held the window open I crawled through and jumped down, landing hard on my feet.

We were in the living room, a tiny square room with just a paisley chesterfield and a plush chair. Empty shelves lined all four walls. The only thing of interest we could see was a small table out in the hallway. On it was a stack of letters held together with a fat elastic band. Zvi stepped carefully to the hall, but try as he might he couldn't prevent the floorboards from squeaking with every step he took. I shuffled to the table and flicked through the envelopes. They all had little coats of arms or fleurs-de-lis in the top left-hand corners. I'd seen enough envelopes like them at home to know they were from the Montréal and Québec governments. About a dozen letters were from the Ministère de Transport and others were from the Roads Department.

Zvi was looking up the staircase. "Want to go up?" he asked without turning around.

"If you want to."

"Sure."

The stairs were incredibly creaky in spite of the thin carpet. We ascended slowly.

The wallpaper was pink and striped with rows of roses, and a small painting of some European-looking town hung straight from a thin, slightly bent nail. The stairs rose to a small landing and blank wall that inched toward us. No matter how gently we put our weight on each step we made a heart-chilling racket.

*"Qui est-ce?"*

We looked at each other. It had been a woman's voice, or something close to it, and it had come from upstairs.

"Caroline?"

"Oh, man!" Zvi groaned. He turned too quickly and slid more than ran down the stairs. I followed, clutching the banister and rushing up against him. We automatically raced to the door, and were trapped.

"Oh, man!" Zvi's eyes were wide and unfocused. I was in a daze, unable to believe this was anything but a dream.

*"Qui est-ce? Qui est là?"*

We heard footsteps on the floor above. In our panic we kept turning the locked doorknob, then tried to figure out how to unlock it. By the time we remembered the window we could see something dark at the top of the stairs. She was yelling *"Qui est-ce? Qui est-ce?"* over and over again.

"Oh, man!" Zvi said again. We had to go toward the staircase to get to the doorway leading to the living room, and that meant getting nearer to the woman I knew was a witch. We ran forward and veered right without pause.

*"Voleurs!"* the witch screamed as she saw us run by. The last thing I saw before making it into the living room was a small old woman standing at the top of the stairs, in a grey or blue nightgown, waving one cane at us while she leaned on another.

The window was down again, of course, but Zvi managed to push it up and scramble to safety. The old lady was still yelling *"Voleurs!"* and I heard creaking that meant she was coming down after me. I thought she looked frail, weak, but obviously she wasn't as weak as she seemed. I had no idea what power she had, what she could do to me. I slid the window up and climbed out, in time to see Zvi jump to the other side of the fence. Just before I let go of the window I heard a sick-sounding *clumph* and a low moan from the stairs.

I didn't see Zvi at all as I ran home, feeling my heart punching the inside of my chest. My lungs were stinging but I kept running, not daring to look back.

The first thing my mother did when I got home was scream at me for making a mess of my pants and shoes. Near one knee the cloth was showing the first signs of tearing.

"Your new birthday pants! Already!"

I couldn't tell her what had happened; she wouldn't believe me about the witch, and wouldn't care.

"You think your grandmother's made of money?"

She sent me to my room and didn't give me any of the lemon cream pie after supper.

I was sure that I'd never sleep again. And I thought I'd never have the nerve to go out on Hallowe'en because she'd fly by and do something to me in revenge. I kept hearing that *clumph*, over and over, and wondered what could have happened, and how I would pay for it.

But I did fall asleep that night. On Hallowe'en Zvi and I, and a couple of my other friends, pulled the thin elastics of our masks over our heads and went out in our black, orange, and red costumes, drawing expressions of terror from our neighbours, and handfuls of candy dropped into our shopping bags; no one dared to deny us.

And during recess Zvi and I bragged in the schoolyard about our meeting with the witch. It became a story we told with delicious horror as often as possible, watching our friends' eyes widen with vicarious thrills.

I never forgot the sound. In fact, it became clearer and clearer over time, eluding my mother's powers of order and correction.

# Living Room

It was at Hebrew School that I first learned all about the Holocaust. I'd seen the old films on TV—the ones that showed bodies being bulldozed and people who were almost skeletons being given metal cups of water to drink—and my parents had mentioned things now and then that I barely understood. In fact, until I was seven or eight I thought Hitler was still alive. But it was Rabbi Friedman who I first heard use the word "Holocaust," and he told us the whole story, about anti-Semitism, the Nazis, the Final Solution.

Hebrew School was every Tuesday and Thursday at 3:45 and a bunch of us from Bedford School—Jeffrey Gold, Wayne Fischman, Zvi Rosen, and I—took the bus right after regular school and then walked down to Mackenzie where the shul was. It was strange going from one school to the other; things were done very differently by the Protestant School Board of Greater Montréal and at Beth Hamedrash. For one thing, Miss Shaw stayed behind her desk most of the time, seldom crossing the invisible line separating it and the blackboard from us. But Rabbi Friedman walked up and down the rows of old metal desks (so ugly compared to Bedford's polished wooden ones) in the dark, stuffy basement classroom, as he told us the stories of Purim and Hanukah. Also, Miss Shaw was strict, meaning she almost never smiled or tried to be nice, and she often punished people without finding out whether they really did what she accused them of. Rabbi Friedman, though, always used a friendly voice, and kept making jokes, trying to entertain us; maybe he knew how hard it was for us to sit through another hour-and-a-half of school, or that we were only there to learn enough Hebrew to get us through our Bar Mitzvahs.

It was the Six Day War that got him to talk about the Holocaust. When the war broke out he brought in a radio so we could listen to the news and cheer on Abba Eban as he tore into our enemies at the United Nations. We wondered why the Arabs wanted so badly to push us out of our thin strip of land and into the sea when they had miles and miles of desert— which they were too stupid or lazy to make bloom as we had done. We had all the proof we needed that God was on our side when little Israel beat the big Arab countries in only one week. After the Arabs surrendered, Rabbi Friedman spent a whole class talking about the 1930s, about the Allies' naïveté, about how the Jews had been the best German citizens but were blamed for all of Germany's problems anyway, about *lebensraum*. The Germans claimed they needed more room to live, so they just took it from everybody else. Hitler persecuted us, but like the Arabs, got just what he deserved in the end.

When I got home I asked my mother whether anyone in our family had been in the war. It was thrilling to think some-one I knew might have been part of all that suffering and hor-ror. She didn't answer me right away, but kept sliding the iron over one of my father's shirts and standing it up at the end of the board, where it made a hiss-sucking sound. The finished clothes lay folded and in a neat pile on the kitchen table.

"Well," she said at last, "Daddy and I both grew up here."
I rolled my eyes at her insistence on continuing to call him
"Daddy" to me; if my sister wanted to keep calling him that,
that was her business. "Your zaidies and bubbies were already
here, before the war." The clothes smelled warm and clean,
and I couldn't resist putting my hand on them; I took it off
again before she had a chance to tell me to. "Actually, Daddy's
parents settled in Chicago."

"I know." I knitted my brow in disappointment. "You
mean, nobody?"

She shrugged, her shoulders lifting the light-grey duster she
wore when she did the laundry or cooking. "Your cousins?
Ruth and her family also grew up in Montréal. Just down the
street from me, in fact, on Jeanne-Mance . . ."

"Yeah." She'd told me that often enough.

She folded up the last shirt and added it to the pile without
saying anything more. I got down from the chair I'd been
kneeling on and went into my room. It was unbelievable: my
family had spent the war here, comfortable and safe, far from
where all the important things were happening, in Europe.
Europe to me was a black-and-white world, which I knew
about mainly from the documentaries about the war, or Walter
Cronkite's *The Twentieth Century*. The sun seldom shone
there, and when it did it wasn't as bright as it was in Canada.
And whatever buildings remained standing were old and dirty,
ready to collapse and disintegrate into a cloud of dust.

When Rabbi Friedman translated *lebensraum*, it reminded me
of my Aunt Ellen's living room. Actually, Aunt Ellen's house
was little more than a living room to me, since that was almost
all I ever saw of it. She lived in the ground-floor flat of a duplex
in my parents' old neighbourhood, although I never found out
exactly where. There was a kitchen I'd gone into once, with

black pans hanging on nails in the walls and a glaringly white stove you lit with a long match. And there was also a bathroom that had an ugly toilet with a smooth, wooden handle at the end of a chain suspended from the ceiling. The sink was terrible; it had separate cold and hot-water taps so you couldn't adjust the temperature of the water when you washed your hands.

But mostly I saw the living room. My sister and I sat on a short chesterfield by the window, while my parents sat on the long chesterfield by the archway leading into the room and talked to my aunt in Hungarian. She would sit unmoving in the dark red paisley chair opposite us, leaning toward them and listening quietly to whatever they said. All I could do was look around the room, at the tiny black ceramic poodle on the swirl-decorated stand beside our chesterfield, or the collection of china figurines dressed in eighteenth-century clothes in the hutch. Beside the lounging ladies and suitors in wide-skirted coats were little photographs in black frames, of relatives who meant nothing to me. Each was half-hidden by glare coming off its protective glass. In fact, everything in the room seemed to be made of either glass or china, and we were told constantly to be careful.

We would arrive at two or three o'clock, and after greeting my parents Aunt Ellen would rest her palm lightly on the left side of my sister's chin, and then mine, smiling all the time; her hand smelled of Nivea cream, the same stuff my mother used. She'd tell us in Hungarian to go into the living room, and my sister and I would obey as if the weird sounds (which I once described to my mother as "tonguey") made perfect sense to us. After talking to my parents for a while she would go into the kitchen to bring in the crumbly little cookies she always made for us. Each had a spot of dried jelly on top, of indeterminable flavour. They were very hard, but at least they were sweet. She offered them to us out of an old, round tin decorated with lacy designs and more eighteenth-century people. I had learned long ago to take only two or three cookies, to avoid getting poked by Sheila.

"You're such a pig!"

"Am not."

"Are too. Mommy!"

Then my parents and Aunt Ellen would begin talking, and Sheila and I would have to sit there waiting for them to finish. I'd run my finger along the smooth lines in the chesterfield's upholstery, occasionally tracing a line down between the arm and cushion where I trapped my finger in the soft roughness; or I'd look at the old-fashioned black clock with gold numbers that hung above the bookshelf near my aunt's chair; it ticked loudly instead of humming inconspicuously like the electric clock in our kitchen.

Finally, when I thought I couldn't stand another minute of listening to Hungarian and that clock, my father would get up and begin the process of leaving. Even when we were in the hallway they continued to talk for what seemed like hours, while I transferred my weight from foot to foot. More smiles and chin-cuppings, and then we would leave at last, as Aunt Ellen waved to us from the doorway like a little girl.


The Friday after Rabbi Friedman talked about the Holocaust I went straight to Jeffrey Gold's house after school, not bothering to get permission first since I had all weekend to do my homework, and I knew how much my mother hated it when I played in the woods near Jeffrey's house. She was sure I'd break my neck falling out of a tree, or get a stick in the eye. But of course the dangers, the chance for adventure, were the whole point. We ran across his backyard to the fence separating the yard from the woods beyond, then jammed our shoes into the narrow spaces between the fence pickets and in one motion propelled ourselves to the leaf-covered ground on the other side.

"I found some more wood," Jeffrey said, pulling up a board he'd hidden under a bush near the fence. One of the board's long edges was badly decayed, but the other was pretty straight and smooth. "I found it over there."

"Is that your property?" I imagined the owner of some nearby duplex catching him and calling the police.

"I don't know," he said, shrugging. "Nobody saw, anyways." I helped him carry the board over to where the others were nailed across the gap between two thin trees. We were building a fort or clubhouse—we weren't sure which. "If we nail it to that one and that one," he said, pointing to another slightly thicker tree that formed a decent triangle with the first two, "we could make part of a good wall."

"It'd be kind of small."

"So?" He tried positioning it. "We aren't going to get a lot of wood, you know." He said things like that in a tone that implied you really should know. "Okay, get the tool box." From beneath another bush I pulled out the small, oval basket we'd found in the woods. On one side of it was a picture of a peach and Fruites Fraîches DuMO on what was left of the label. We'd collected at least a dozen nails and screws—some slightly bent—as well as thumbtacks and pieces of hardware we couldn't identify. We also had a hammer I'd found in a drawer at home. "Now, hold it here," he said. I held the board against the tree, stiffening my arm and planting my foot in the dirt as he tried to bang in a nail.

"Ow! Jeez!" He'd hit the board so hard it jumped in my hands, and a sliver of rotten wood stuck under my fingernail. I pulled the sliver out, letting the board clatter to the ground.

"Hey, watch it!" Jeffrey looked at my finger. "Is it bleeding?"

"Yeah." I watched, fascinated, as the dark liquid welled up

under my nail and began oozing out. I took a Kleenex from my pocket and pressed it against my fingernail, wincing at the throbbing pain. The board lay by my feet, one end barbed with the now-bent nail. We sat down on the other end, careful not to damage our school pants. All that blood was gloriously horrific, like Hallowe'en.

"Did your grandparents or anyone get killed by Hitler?" I asked, smoothing the darkly stained Kleenex out.

"What?" He thought for a while. "No, I don't think so. Why? Who said they were?"

"Nobody. Just asking." It seemed so weird; all those people killed but I couldn't find anyone who'd actually been there, actually seen it happen. What had Rabbi Friedman been talking about? "You mean, nobody was in a concentration camp or anything?"

"No! Why d'you keep asking?"

"Just wondering."

"What about you?"

"Nobody."

"At all? Not even your weird aunt?"

"Her?" I tried to remember what my mother had said. "No . . . and she's not weird. Just boring. She doesn't speak English."

Jeffrey stood up. "At all?"

"Nope." I tried pulling the Kleenex away but a small disk of fibres remained stuck to the end of my finger.

"Is it okay?"

"Yeah, yeah." The Kleenex was stiff and badly stained, but I was sure the bleeding had stopped. I kept thinking back to my mother's answers.

"Then come on. Help me with this damn board." I stood, and he pulled the board up. "Does it hurt?"

"It's okay!" I used my other fingers to grip the clean edge of the board while he hammered in two more nails out of our diminishing supply. He banged the nails flat, denting the wood a little. The wall didn't look very good at all—the boards weren't flush at all as they followed the curves of the trees—but I wasn't going to say anything.

He stood back, trying to find an angle at which it would look impressive. "Great, eh?" he said. "It'll soon be finished, and we won't even need to put a roof on because of the branches and leaves and stuff. We can finish it when school's over."

"What? Yeah."

"You going to Expo?" he asked. I nodded, barely paying attention. "You going to see the Israel pavilion? I am."

"Yeah." We hid the tool box in its usual place, then stepped up onto the crossbeam running across the backs of the pickets and jumped over them onto the lawn.

"It's late. I got to go."

"Okay. You coming tomorrow? Maybe we can look around for more wood."

"Sure. See you."

"See you."

I scooped up my schoolbag from the driveway and rushed home. I got there before five; my sister was sitting on the chesterfield in her navy tunic watching TV. I went to my room to drop off my bag, then to the bathroom to wash my finger. On the way I passed the kitchen where I saw my mother bending down to look through the window in the oven door. Instead of saying "Hi" I kept going, and in the bathroom turned on both taps to get the water to a comfortable temperature. I washed off most of the blood and Kleenex until all that was left was a dirty-looking crescent under my nail. I went into the living room to catch the beginning of *I Love Lucy*.

"Aren't you supposed to do your homework before you watch TV?" Sheila said as I sat down on the floor beside the chesterfield.

"It's Friday."

"So?"

"So you're supposed to change when you get home."

She rolled her eyes and sighed.

I'd seen this episode many times before, and I wasn't concentrating anyway because I was listening for the downstairs door to open. We lived on the top floor of a duplex, and when the downstairs door opened it grunted loudly and the upstairs one rattled in the draft. My mother came out of the kitchen and stopped when she saw me.

"Oh! Hi, Lawrence," she said.

"Hi," I said without looking away from the TV. I could feel her eyes on me but I didn't look back; finally, she returned to the kitchen.

When the two doors sounded I got up and waited in the hall right in front of the door. I listened anxiously to my father's distinctive loud, slow walk up those speckled-stone steps, both afraid and impatient for him to come up. He opened the upstairs door and his eyes widened a little when he saw me standing there.

"Hi, Lar," he said. "What's up?" I followed him to the closet, watching as he put his hat up on the top shelf and slid his briefcase under the coats. When he straightened up he began twirling his short, curly hair around his finger—as he did whenever he was wondering about something—the sleeve of his jacket bunching up around the shoulder. My mother stood in the kitchen doorway, arms crossed. "Everything okay, Lar?" my father asked.

"Was Aunt Ellen in the war?"

"Yeah." He looked over my head at my mother. I turned and saw her frown at him. "Why?"

"What happened to her?"

"Well, I don't know all the details, really. She doesn't talk about it much."

"Don't bother Daddy," my mother said, and then pointed warningly at me. "Or your aunt. That kind of thing you shouldn't talk about."

"Well . . ." my father began, but my mother cut him off.

"Why would you want to know about such things?" she asked.

I shrugged and said: "Okay, okay." That seemed to satisfy her; she went up to give my father his kiss, and neither of them mentioned it again, even when we were all sitting around the kitchen table having supper. After supper, as always, my father watched Pulse News on CFCF, then went into his bedroom to sit in the armchair and read one of his science fiction books.

I didn't bother going back to Jeffrey's on Saturday because the fort was turning out so badly I didn't see any point wasting more time on it. Then on Sunday I actually looked forward to going to Aunt Ellen's; I wanted to see her, look at her more closely, now that I knew all about her. We got ready in the usual way: my mother bought a box of assorted danish at Cantor's; I put on a school jersey and good pants, my sister the dress she wore to parties and shul, and my father a suit and white shirt, but no tie. Just before we left my mother ran her stiff brush over my scalp, and licked a handkerchief to wipe away some dirt under my eye.

"Are you going to behave yourself?"

I nodded. Whenever she asked a question like that her eyes showed real worry, as if I was bound to do something awful. She never went into hysterics the way Wayne Fischman's mother did; every time I went to Wayne's his mother would panic: "Did you tell your mother you were coming? Don't make a mess! You sure you told your mother?" I felt sorry for Wayne, although he just laughed at her, and actually called her crazy—something I found incredible. My mother was never that bad, but she would give me a hard look, which I resented. What had I ever done to deserve that much suspicion? Had I ever stolen anything? Cheated at school? It wasn't fair.

We got into our four-door Austin, which smelled of oil and old leather, and my mother put the white cardboard Cantor's box on my lap. I ran my fingers around the tight string binding it, making a half-hearted effort to untangle its multi-layered knot as we drove. To get to Aunt Ellen's we had to pass through my parents' old neighbourhood. Marie-Anne . . . Jeanne-Mance . . . Mount Royal . . . every time we went to Aunt Ellen's my mother would point out the streets and tell my sister and me about them.

"I can't believe they tore down that building. My friend Rachel lived there as long as I can remember."

"That's where my father used to buy us soda. Five cents if you wanted syrup. Two cents for plain."

The long, black alleys and grey balconies, sheds, and fences looked ancient. A skinny cat watched our car, then shot off through the opening in a high, wooden fence. We passed a fish store that reeked; old ladies dressed in black and men with moustaches came out of it carrying damp, brown paper parcels. The stores had signs in Greek as well as English, and on most signs the bizarre geometric letters were bigger than the familiar ones. I silently urged my father to hurry up, hating the red lights that caught us.

My father parked around the corner from my aunt's place. As we got out we were watched by a man sitting on the black iron stairs curving up the front of his building. Even though it wasn't all that warm, he was wearing a sleeveless undershirt and was smoking a cigarette mostly hidden between his thumb and forefinger. All the buildings here had front doors flush with the cement walks, and concrete alleys, but—as far as I knew—no backyards.

My aunt's building had no walk at all; the door was right

out at the sidewalk. As always, it took my aunt a long time to answer the buzzer, long enough to make you think she wasn't home. But then the little lace curtain in the door's small square of glass fluttered slightly, and the door eased open. She stood looking at us as if our presence there was a surprise. Then she nodded and pulled the door wider, shifting her cane from one hand to the other as we went in. My mother took the box of danish from my hand and held it out to her, then put it on the short wooden stand in the hallway. It would stay there till we left—my mother never let her serve any to us.

My aunt smiled and nodded. *"Köszönöm, köszönöm szépen; nem kellett volna."*

My mother answered with something I could tell from her gestures meant "It's nothing."

I stared up at Aunt Ellen as I passed, and she smiled down at me. My father and mother took turns kissing her on the cheek, then my aunt put her hand on my sister's chin and mine, saying, *"Kinder, kinder."* Without waiting for our signal I went to take my seat in the living room and Sheila followed. Beside our chesterfield the little black poodle was in its usual place, next to the miniature tin bowl and spoon; the gold lettering on the books in the shelf caught the dim sunlight that came through the filmy curtains behind us.

But I wasn't interested in looking at all the fragile things in the room. Instead, as my aunt entered I watched her face, focusing on her eyes. In the movies the concentration camp victims always looked into the cameras with huge eyes set in their bony faces. But her eyes were narrow and had soft bags under them. She lowered herself into the dark red chair, propping her cane against the wall and bookcase. She listened intently to what my father was telling her, one hand on top of the other that rested gently on the arm of her chair. She sat motionless, not even rustling her print dress or shifting her thick black shoes. And when she nodded she did so slowly, easily. After talking to my father for a while she turned and said something to me and Sheila.

"She wants to know whether you'd like your cookies now," my father translated.

Sheila and I both nodded.

"*Igen,*" my father relayed to her, stretching his arm over the top of the chesterfield. Aunt Ellen pushed herself up and shuffled to the kitchen, not bothering to take her cane but leaning on the walls. I looked at the painting that hung above my parents: it showed a calm, dark blue lake with tiny white sailboats making "V"s in the water, and green and yellow hills in the background. I took a deep breath.

"Dad," I said finally, "can I ask her?"

My father gave me a look I didn't quite understand; my mother glared and clutched her purse tightly. Aunt Ellen was already standing just beyond the archway, and her eyes were on me, too. I suppose it was the first time I'd ever said anything in her house above a whisper.

"Lawrence!" my mother hissed.

Aunt Ellen came in and asked my father something as she put the round tin on the coffee table. His answer was long, so I figured he was telling her everything that I wanted to ask her. But her expression didn't change. She sat down, leaning slightly towards me, with her hands, as before, on the arm of her chair. "You ask," she said to me, nodding and smiling encouragingly.

I blinked. "She knows English?"

"Not much." My mother was about to say something but my father put his hand on her arm. I could feel Sheila sitting scandalized beside me; I knew she was rolling her eyes. "Ask her anyway. She wants you to." He fiddled with his hair, elbow resting on the top of the chesterfield. Now I couldn't speak at all. "Don't be scared."

"Were you in the war?"

*"Igen,"* she said, nodding slowly.

"Like, in a concentration camp?"

My mother said, "Oy" quietly and looked away; my aunt consulted my father. He couldn't possibly have translated it properly; her face didn't change at all. She still had the half-smile, even as she turned back to me and shook her head. *"Nem.* No." She struggled to find the word. "Ghetto."

"Oh."

I looked off to the side, trying to figure this out, and the glare from the hutch caught the corner of my eye. I'd expect-ed—I'd wanted—to find all the horror, the pain, that I'd been told about; to touch it. But it didn't seem to be here, or even be real. Had any of it really happened? What had my mother been afraid for me to hear? Looking at Aunt Ellen, who calmly wait-ed for me, I was sure now that the films hadn't told me every-thing either.

Still, though she hadn't gone through all that suffering, at least she had been in the war. I'd be able to find out something, even if it was as bland as my mother's stories about the neigh-bourhood. "Well, what was it like?" I asked.

Instead of asking for a translation, she got my father to teach her how to say "Very bad."

And she didn't cry, or scream; she just sat there quietly, waiting for more questions.

I sat stunned, no longer knowing what to expect, or believe. I glanced at my mother who looked almost as confused as I was.

I shrugged to indicate that I had nothing more to ask. Aunt Ellen stood up and carried the tin over to us. I only took one cookie out of the tin. She laughed quietly and took out anoth-er one, which she put in my hand along with a napkin. She returned to her chair, and after a few seconds of silence she and my father started talking again as if nothing had happened.

Later, my father stood up and we all moved out of the living room. I'd eaten the first cookie, but kept the other wrapped up in the napkin, holding it lightly because my finger still hurt a bit. Aunt Ellen motioned for me to put the cookie in my pocket. As we stood in the hallway she rested her palm on my chin first, and said: *"Kinder, kinder."*

I kept looking at her as we walked out. She stood in the doorway, waving to us like a little girl as we walked to the car.

# Short Cut

As far as I was concerned, the neighbourhood I grew up in was divided into two distinct worlds. One was made up of the sidewalks and front yards of Goyer Street; my school was straight down the street, and each day I walked along the familiar concrete of the sidewalk between the rows of duplexes and apartment buildings that were fronted by small lawns bisected by short walks. Beside the duplex stairs were rock gardens: patches of blue, yellow, and white flowers bunched together, and shimmering green moss coating smooth, grey boulders.

The other world was in the backyards, like my own, and those behind the buildings on the north side of Goyer where I sometimes took my short cut to school during the fall and spring. I learned about short cuts from my school readers: a short cut was tough to travel, and went through unknown, maybe dangerous terrain. Most of the backyards on my route had simple wooden fences that I could climb without too much trouble, although I had to return to the street to go around the huge pool fence behind one building. But as soon as I was by it, I ran down the next driveway to continue my short cut, trying to make up for lost time by running across the lawns. It didn't bother me that taking my short cut probably took longer than using Goyer Street. It was the difficulty of the route, and the fact that it was more interesting and exciting than the sidewalk. And the backyards on both sides of the street abutted onto strips of wooded wilderness that begged to be explored.


My own backyard was probably the best on Goyer. Beyond the small square of trimmed grass nearest our duplex (with its central patio of grey and white tiles that were never even), the lawn rose sharply up a toboggan-perfect slope, ending in a line of bushes that separated the regular yard from the woods beyond. That whole stretch of woods was paradise. As far as I was concerned it belonged to me, and I refused to let anyone, especially my sister, go up there. Sheila would whine to my mother about it, but they both knew she didn't really want to climb my trees or get speared by bush-twigs. She was just jealous because at least I had a place of my own.

At that time we had to share a room, and we were both getting too old to stand it. Our house did have a spare room, but my father was using it for an office for his extra bookkeeping work, and refused to give it up. My parents kept promising we'd move into a bigger place one day, even a real house, when they could afford it. I didn't want to move, but I also didn't want to put up with my sister any more, and even though our beds were as far from each other as possible—sometimes she experimented with old clothesline and sheets to divide our room in half—we were getting desperate. I was tired of her coming in when I had my soldiers deployed in perfectly straight lines and almost knocking them over as she walked around getting things. I was tired of her exasperated sighs as she did her homework, as if she were the only one who had to do arithmetic problems or history projects. And there were times when I just wanted to lie on my bed, silently, away from the sounds of the TV, the washing machine grinding in the kitchen, my mother talking on the phone to one of her B'nai Brith friends, my father banging on the desk in the office and swearing ("Jesus Murphy!").

At least the kids in the school readers didn't have to share their rooms. I loved those readers, and the cellophane-covered books in the library (a shelf beneath the side blackboard). I savoured the texture of those large-printed words with the pictures they called to mind, even if I found most of what they portrayed totally foreign. Kids in the stories had grandparents who lived on farms, and dogs . . . the only pets we ever had were the goldfish my mother brought home from Woolworth's in plastic bags sagging with water. I wanted some of the things the kids in the books had, and to do what they got to do: help track down criminals, fly spaceships like Tom Swift, Jr., and take thrilling short cuts to town through dark forests full of mystery and adventure. But there were no huge forests nearby, and I felt silly when I first saw the words short cut and all I could think of was my mother's instructions to me whenever I went to the barber-shop in the Wilderton Shopping Centre. "Tell him, short," she'd say, as if there were any other possibility. It was the time of hippies, but I wanted to look like a true boy, like the ones in the books. If teenagers wanted to look like sissies, that was their problem.

One of the books in the library, *The Macmillan Book of Stories for Young People*, had a story about a boy named Tom who'd built a treehouse in the giant oak in his backyard. The illustration showed a neat cube made of planks, complete with door, nestled in the branches of the huge tree. A rough sign saying Clubhouse was nailed above the door.

I realized that if I couldn't get my own room, there was one solution. I wouldn't tell anyone what I was up to, in case they laughed or wanted to interfere; it seemed very important, for some reason, that no one should know about my plans. The idea would be violated somehow if anyone knew.

But I didn't know how to go about building my own house—I had no rules or guidelines to follow. The closest thing I had to a pattern was Howard Cohen's fort, which he'd started to build the previous summer and then abandoned for lack of wood. I figured I'd find plenty of scrap wood in the neighbourhood if I looked hard enough.

The first thing I needed was a tree, of course, and that was the easy part. I had a favourite tree up in the woods behind our house, about half-way between the shrubs on our side and the fences on the Barclay side. It was the thickest tree around, and solid except for a gash in the side where a runaway car had hit it years before after losing its brakes going down a Barclay Street driveway. The gash had healed, and the tree's exposed flesh hardened but the scar was deep, and I worried about the tree's strength. But it was the thickest tree around.


After school and on weekends I collected material. I took my short cut more often, looking for stray boards and beams hidden under the brush in the woods on both sides of Goyer. I couldn't find very much, but did manage to collect a few pieces of wood of different lengths and thicknesses that I might be able to cut and shape with the saw we'd found in our garage when we moved into the duplex. The saw wasn't very sharp, but it was huge and looked capable of cutting through anything. I hid whatever lumber I found on the way to school in order to pick it up on the way home, along with screws and nails (most rusty but usable) I scooped out of the dirt or piles of leaves.

One Thursday I was squatting in the woods behind Kenny Wasserman's house, yanking up a rotten plank mostly buried in the soil, when I heard: "What are you doing?"

Kenny stood over me, hands on knees, looking half-curious, half-belligerent, ready to defend his property if need be.

"Nothing." I hadn't decided yet who would be allowed to use my treehouse, so for now I didn't even want my friends to know about it. Kenny had been my best friend one year, but wasn't now. "I'm just looking for good wood."

"Why? What are you making?"

I looked at Kenny in order to communicate with my expression that I'd told him as much as I was going to. Kenny was not exactly fat, but getting there, and for a second I wanted to push in his wide face for pestering me. But if he didn't actually demand that I either tell him or get off his property, I'd try to ignore him. He watched me tug the board sideways, swinging it back and forth until it broke free.

"It's rotten," he said.

"So?"

He shrugged. "I don't care."

I hoped Kenny's mother would save me by yelling his name from the back balcony. She was always doing that every now and then, no matter where you were in the neighbourhood. You'd hear her voice calling "Kenny! Kenny!" over and over. We made fun of him for it, telling him his mommy was calling him and he should run. But he never did, at least not right away.

He stood stooping over me, watching closely as I lifted the board, or what was left of it, and then banged the dirty end against the ground to jar the moist soil loose.

"It's mine," Kenny said simply.

"No it isn't!" I couldn't believe his gall. "You're mental!"

"It's on my property so it's mine."

"Finders keepers."

"Give it to me; it's mine!" He reached for the bad end, which was still specked with brown and had a pillbug curling around one splinter jutting from the edge.

I pulled the board from his grasp and ran through the woods toward home. He chased me briefly, then gave up, and waved dismissively in my direction.

By that weekend I had a fairly good supply of boards that didn't look very solid or uniform, but that could, I thought, become a reasonable house if properly used. I had nails and screws, too, which I kept in an old fruit basket I'd found long ago. Most of the nails were bent, but I was sure I could use my father's hammer to straighten them out if need be.

I stacked the boards beside my tree, trying to keep the pile from spreading out as it kept wanting to do. Many of the boards were studded with old nails that I couldn't push out, so on Sunday afternoon I took my father's hammer from the second drawer under the kitchen counter to bang most of the nails out. Some were so brown and bent all I could do with them was pound them flat against the wood, and most of the nails I could remove were too warped to be useful.

The tree divided at about chest-level into two main branches that formed a narrow fork. I grabbed the two branches and pulled myself up to stand with one foot wedged in the fork. From here, I could see my whole yard: the lawn, a solid green except for the patio and my red football helmet with the yellow stripe that ran over its centre gleaming in the weak sunlight; the white fence with the curlicue arch over the gate that opened onto the sloping driveway; and straight across from where I stood, our back balcony, where chrome lawn chairs with green and yellow vinyl webbing stood folded and leaning against the brick. The glass in the door and window were both black, revealing nothing of the kitchen beyond. I stood up straighter, straining to see the top of the flat roof, knowing I could never see it, but trying anyway.

I figured the best way to start the treehouse would be to fit a board across the fork, nailing it to both branches to form a base for the floor. Once I got the floor started the rest would be easy, since I'd have a less awkward place to stand as I made the walls. I climbed down and searched among my collection of wood for a board that would fit between the forks at the right height: low enough to reach, high enough to support a good-sized floor. I chose one that seemed right and with the claw of the hammer scraped off an old cocoon that still clung to the underside. I lifted the board into place and tried positioning it between the branches. But I couldn't keep it steady enough to get a nail in place, and I couldn't hold the board, the nail, and the hammer at the same time. I lowered the board to the ground, stood on it with one foot, and banged a large, slightly bent nail into one end just deep enough to hold it. By the time it was that far in, though, the nail was bent even more, and obviously wouldn't survive more hammering. I sighed noisily and yanked it out, scraping the side of my finger on its head. I threw it onto the ground in disgust and decided I'd need to use my best nails for the base; the others would do for the walls.

The second nail began to bend, too, so I pulled it out before it got too wrecked; the third was so big it cracked the end of the board. A clean slit opened from the nail hole right to the board's end, but at least the nail remained straight (or mostly so). I raised the board again, lined it up carefully, and began hammering. The nail was in an awkwardly high position, though, and so I couldn't bring much force down on it. It barely moved even though I hit it with almost every swing. My ears began to ring with the bangs that echoed throughout the neighbourhood. With all the noise I was making I thought the whole world must have known what I was up to by now.

At last, the nail was deep enough into the tree to hold it, but somehow the entire board had pivoted and the other end stuck out in mid-air. When I straightened it out again, the nail loosened a bit, and I saw that I hadn't quite gotten the nail down into the branch. In fact, the bark was threatening to peel away altogether, destroying whatever support the nail had. I rested my forearms on the tree, watching the board return to its out-of-line position as if it had a mind of its own, and I felt like ripping the board out and forgetting the whole stupid idea.

After a few minutes I regained my patience and pivoted the board straight, nailed it to the second branch as well as I could with a strange-looking nail that had almost no head at all, and secured the board at the first end with yet another of my best nails. The board was a little tilted, and the nail shafts were visible between the bottom of the board and the branches, but at least I'd finished the first stage. It was close to supper time, so I dropped the hammer into the toolbox on top of all the other hardware, made my way through my usual gap in the bushes down to the lawn and ran across to my house. As I climbed the black iron staircase I looked back at the tree and saw my board, a shining yellow bar in the darkening green and brown woods.

At supper my father asked: "What was all that banging?"

"Nothing."

He tightened the cap on the ketchup bottle, and some stray ketchup oozed out from under the cap. I looked at the side of my finger, which ached but didn't bleed.

"Making something?"

I shrugged. I was afraid I'd face more questions but my sister began talking about her troubles at Arithmetic, how her teacher never explained things but expected you to just know. I was glad for the interruption and ate my roast chicken without looking up, taking more care than necessary to soak the slices in the ketchup blob on my plate before eating them. I also worked hard with my fork to keep the Niblets from being tainted by stray ketchup because I hated the combination.

But during a pause in Sheila's lament my mother said: "I saw you climbing that tree. I don't like you doing that."

"Why?"

"Because you'll fall and break your neck."

"No I won't!"

She shrugged. "Fine, don't listen to me." I wanted to say something about if I had my own room . . . but kept my mouth shut.

At school the next day I kept my silence, even with Howard Cohen, my best friend. In the schoolyard at recess he showed off his collection of Beatles cards, each a black-and-white photo of one or more Beatles and bearing an autograph print-ed in blue ink. As I thumbed through them, amazed at the Beatles' girly looks, I carefully restrained myself from telling him my secret.

"I've almost got the whole set," he said, "but my father won't give me any more money."

To me, Howard was the embodiment of poverty. My par-ents could never refuse my requests for card money, field trips, or anything else, but he was always talking about how much he couldn't afford. I didn't know why his family had no money, but it had something to do with the fact his mother no longer lived at home. At least I was secure in the knowledge that some day I'd be able to move into a house; Howard would probably spend the rest of his life in a duplex. I knew he'd appreciate my treehouse more than anyone, but I didn't want to reveal any-thing yet, and anyway his being poor wasn't my fault. Some day I would let him come to my treehouse—just not yet.

"Why do you want Beatles cards anyway?" I asked. "They look stupid."

He shrugged; obviously he'd never thought about it. "I like them."

I shook my head. How could anyone like that loud music, that hair hanging past the ears? The whole world seemed to be going crazy. On TV teenagers were shown running around with long hair, doing violent, shocking things: rioting, taking drugs. When the Beatles first came on *The Ed Sullivan Show,* my grandmother was visiting for one of her occasional Sunday dinners, and my whole family looked on in horror as those weird creatures screamed and scraped their guitars to the tearful ecstasy of teenage girls who screamed back. When my grandmother said: "What are they, girls?" I had to agree; at least I knew how hair was supposed to look, even if some of my friends were starting to actually like the music played by those ridiculous-looking groups. I gave up on Howard and went to watch the champ game in progress on the other side of the yard. If I were building a whole world and not just a house, I thought, I'd get rid of all the crazy teenagers, or at least teach them how they were supposed to act.

After school I rushed home, changed into my play pants and shoes, and went out back to work on the treehouse. First, I got the saw out of the garage. I'd need to cut the floor planks to uniform lengths, a job that I figured wouldn't take too long. Meanwhile, Sheila was in the driveway with Tammy Abromovitch, her best friend, drawing a hopscotch court on the pavement with a tiny piece of white chalk. As I carried the saw down the driveway to the gate leading to the backyard, I gave Sheila and her game a wide berth. She had her own place to play, I thought; why would she ever need mine?

Up in the woods, I gathered the thinnest, least-warped boards and lay them side by side. I knew the boards weren't the same length and that I'd have to cut them, but now I realized that no two boards were the same thickness either, so no matter what I did, the floor would be very uneven. With the shortest of the boards as my guide, I began sawing off the end of the next-shortest piece, using a carefully piled stack of wood as my horse. At first the sawing went quickly, but it wasn't long before the saw jammed inside the groove. I had to keep working it loose to make another thrust or two. The sawing was easiest when I worked at a corner, but whenever I tried sawing straight up and down or across the top of the board, I got almost nowhere.

"I knew you were making something."

I looked up. Kenny stood in the woods not far from me. A wall of tall shrubs separated our backyard from our neighbours', ending where the woods began. If you extended the line of shrubs into the woods, Kenny was standing right on the line, careful not to cross the boundary onto our property.

"What is it?" he asked.

"I told you. Nothing."

He surveyed the work I'd already done, and the stack of wood at my feet. "You're making a treehouse."

I couldn't think of a lie. "So?"

"You stole our wood."

"No, I didn't. You weren't using it."

After a pause he said: "Can I play in it?"

"It's mine. It's not a clubhouse or like that."

He made a mean face. "Then you can't play with my chemistry set again."

That wasn't a fair retaliation, but before I could say anything his mother began calling him. "Kenny! Kenny!"

"Your mommy's calling. Why don't you go home or you'll get a spanking?"

He hesitated, then ran as fast as he could through the woods and disappeared, and I dismissed him as a big baby.

I went back to my sawing with renewed energy. The sky was darkening quickly, but I finally got to the end of the first piece. As I reached the edge, that entire side splintered, and I had to cut through dangerous-looking spears of wood before I got the end completely sawed off. The result was a plank with a slightly angled, very jagged end that only matched up with my shortest floorboard on one side. Even then, the two planks were noticeably uneven in thickness. But at least I'd made a start, although at this rate my treehouse would take a year, and nothing like the week or two that Tom took to make his.

I raised my guide board up and banged a nail into it and through the support, which barely clung to the branches, twice almost giving way entirely under the hammering. Somehow, the first floorboard held, although it was a bit tilted (along with the support) and not quite centred. I nailed the second board flush against the first—not lined up exactly—but close enough, and I thought I could always saw off the extra bits at both ends later. As I positioned the board for the final hammering I got a nasty splinter in the base of my thumb. I tried to ignore the oozing blood. It was hard to forget all the times my mother had warned me about getting an infection. It was starting to get too dark to work, so I put my tools into the toolbox and went home for supper.

My mother was in the kitchen setting out the dishes, giving each a wipe with the hem of her duster before laying it on the table. When I came in she said: "Working hard out there?"

"Yeah," I said warily.

"You love that backyard, eh?"

I nodded. I remembered her saying once that the backyard was the one thing my parents had most liked about this duplex in the first place. And I played in the woods a lot, especially in the summer when the leaves hid me from the house, where I could believe I was far from home.

"I may have a lemon for you," she said, but made no move towards the drawer near the fridge. She bought lemon juice for her tea in containers shaped like lemons, and when they were empty they made perfect water canteens, even if they were a bit small. "What are you doing up there, anyway?"

"Nothing. Stuff."

She looked at me briefly, then turned away. My father was sitting on the living room couch reading *The Star*, with one leg crossed over the other and holding his ankle in place. My sister sat on the floor in front of the TV watching *Mike Douglas*. When my father saw me come in he said: "Hey, workman!"

"Hi."

"I heard you banging again. Don't lose the hammer, eh?"

"I won't."

"Is it still a secret what you're building?"

Even telling him it was a secret seemed like revealing too much; I just wanted everyone to forget about it.

"It's just a thing for me," I said, then went to my room—or at least my half of the room.

My family didn't let up on me during supper, either. My father said, "You got all kinds of wood up there, eh?"

"Yeah." I spooned up my chicken noodle soup and blew away the steam.

"I heard. He's building a treehouse," my sister said, then looked at me as if she'd won some sort of contest. "Right?"

"Is that it?" my mother asked. "A treehouse?"

I ate non-committally.

"A big one?" Sheila asked, and I knew what she was getting at. I feared my parents would make me let her use it, too.

"No, just big enough for one person."

My mother ladled goulash onto my father's plate before finally sitting down at her own place. "How come? Don't you want your friends to play there?"

I sighed. "It's just for me."

"How come?" she repeated. Why did she keep asking? Why was it was so important to her? "I mean, what are you building it for?"

"'Cause I'm getting out of here," I said.

I'm not sure exactly what I meant by that, or what I meant most by it. For one thing, I meant that I had to get out of the house, away from the crowding. This was my mother's house more than mine, and I needed my own room. I also meant that we were going to move anyway, so why should I have to put up with sharing a room while we still lived here? And I meant that she ought to be happy I'd be out of her hair more.

But instead of being happy she just looked at me, quietly, for a few seconds. My father and sister kept eating, not realizing anything was wrong. I saw my mother's lips narrow briefly, then her face softened again and she moved her fork through the goulash on her plate. She didn't talk to me again all supper long. I couldn't imagine what I'd said wrong, and wouldn't ask. But everything seemed to be okay later, so I didn't worry too much about it.


The next afternoon I made another floorboard. The plank that was closest in length and thickness to the others was almost unmanageably heavy, as if made of concrete. By now I knew enough to draw a pencil line across the rougher end, as a guide for my saw, using my dullest pencil so I wouldn't risk ruining one I'd just sharpened for school. I started in with the saw, but the board was as hard as it was heavy; after more than an hour of pushing and pulling, I'd barely gotten halfway through the board.

In frustration I yanked the saw out of its shallow groove and threw it into a bush, where it hung swaying on the bunched, thin branches. The tiny, young leaves couldn't quite hide it from my sight. The thin black slit I'd made across the board stared up at me, tempting me to go on. But there was no point; even if I managed to cut through the board completely, I was well inside my pencilled line, so the board was already ruined. And even if it wasn't completely useless, it was much too thick to match the other floorboards.

I then looked at my wood collection and realized I'd never have enough to make a complete treehouse, certainly nothing like the one in the book. If I had enough for walls, I wouldn't have enough for a roof of any kind. And how would I cut out windows? Or a door? Tom, I remembered, had had his father's help—but that contradicted the whole point of building the treehouse.

I looked up at the floor I'd made so far, which almost, but not quite, spanned the fork in the tree trunk. One more board would fill that gap, and at least produce something finished, complete. So I yanked the saw from the bush's tangles and started from the other end of the board, beginning at the pencil line and keeping the saw angled as I'd now learned to do. It was dark by the time I got through to the cut I'd begun on the other side, and the unwanted endpiece twisted, snapped, and hung down by a few splinters. I cut through them and exhaustedly watched the endpiece fall to the ground.

I heaved the board into place and nailed it down. The brace supporting it held firm, as if it had become part of the tree. I knew now that I needed more than two branches to hold up a treehouse, and I knew I could only stand directly over the support or the whole thing would come down. But it didn't matter: I'd just have to balance myself carefully.

I grabbed the branches and pulled myself up onto the floor, then stood with my feet aligned with the brace underneath. The floor held—even when I slowly shifted my weight to the sides to test its strength—and felt a rush of satisfaction. I couldn't go too far from the middle of the floor without hearing some dangerous tearing sounds from underneath, but the floor was much steadier than I'd expected.

Keeping my feet wide apart, I stood motionless and looked out through the trees and bushes. The light was on in our kitchen. The walls of my duplex were now a dark purple, the sky above a deep blue, like the Sea Blue crayons I used to have, but the kitchen glowed through the window and door. I could see my mother moving back and forth between the stove and the table.

I stood watching for what seemed like hours. For some reason I felt like crying. I wanted to be inside, but I also didn't want to go, not yet . . . I saw my father come into the kitchen and talk to my mother for a few moments, before disappearing as he sat down at the kitchen table. I continued watching, my chest aching. I was usually already sitting at the table when my father came in from watching the news on TV. But this time I'd be late.

# Man and His World

I'll always think of the 1960s as the age of science fiction. The future was everywhere. It wasn't just the many science fiction movies and TV shows that came out, though that was a big part of it. *Star Trek*, *2001*, and my favourite, *Lost in Space* . . . they all portrayed a future that was clean, bright, exciting. Buildings would be huge, sparkling with steel and glass; there's always be enough to eat and robots to do the dirty work. We'd have flying cars, picturephones, and three-dimensional TV.

I could see the future on the covers of my father's books and magazines, too. He belonged to the Science Fiction Book Club, and the covers of the books he'd pull from the cardboard packages were full of aliens, or shining spaceships flying over Earth (with the Western Hemisphere clearly outlined beneath), or just bizarre shapes and angled lettering that were intriguing enough.

He also bought issues of *Fantasy and Science Fiction* and *Amazing*, which he kept in a cardboard box from Steinberg's under his bed. He'd turn on the lamp on his nightstand and read in the armchair beside the bed, spinning some of his curly hair around his finger as he often did when he was concentrating on something.

But even beyond the science-fiction shows, the comic books, my father's books and magazines, people everywhere were looking forward to a shining and inevitable new world. Music, hairstyles, attitudes: everything was changing. As a kid I had no idea what the world would be like when I grew up. Could rock music and hair get any crazier? When the hippies took over, would we all be on drugs? I did know the world would be one of vivid colours, like the psychedelic designs on the covers of the albums my sister began to collect. We didn't have a colour TV, but it wasn't hard to tell what the *Laugh-In* set looked like; even Ed Sullivan changed to a mod set to attract teenagers.

Of course, the space flights made it more certain than anything that the pictures we got from science fiction were bound to come true—it was just a matter of time. My family would sit in front of the TV watching every lift-off (a term more scientific than blast-off), and I silently counted down with the announcer. Then the tall white rocket puffed smoke, hesitated, and finally left the ground as everyone knew it would. There was even more fire spewing out of the Gemini rocket engines than they ever put on the covers of my Tom Swift, Jr. books or the novels and magazines my father read, but that was only because our rockets were so primitive. In time, people would be taking sleek silver spaceships all over the solar system.

The one place where I saw the future come to life, and all my science fiction images made real, was Expo '67. My father was sure we'd want to go almost every weekend, so he got a season's passport. On *Pulse News* we watched the progress of the construction as the weird, futuristic pavilions rose from man-made islands. Building the islands, we were told, was very expensive, but nobody seemed to mind too much. What did money matter when you were building the future? After all, people would be landing on the moon soon. They even had a ride at La Ronde, the amusement park, called The Gyratron, which the news announcer said would be like riding a spaceship into the mouth of a monster. I was determined to take that ride before doing anything else at Expo, if my parents let.

My father got the passport through a friend of his I'd only seen two or three times before. Jack was the epitome of the early 1960s man to me: tall, balding, wearing horn-rimmed glasses—like Mel Cooley on *The Dick Van Dyke Show*. He was the sort of businessman that hippies were always making fun of. But I didn't know whether Jack actually worked in an office, or what he did. He came one Sunday in May to bring the passport and discuss something with my father, who told my mother to keep us kids out of the way. It sounded very important, and my father was as excited as I'd ever seen him.

"Hey, Sport," Jack said to me as he climbed the stairs of our duplex. I held the upper door open against the draft.

"Hi." I tolerated his calling me "Sport" even though I knew no reason for him to do it.

"Your dad home?" Jack had a voice like a radio announcer's, and I thought it was marvellous.

"Sure."

My mother came out of the kitchen, wiping her hands on the bottom of her apron. "Hello, Jack," she said. "Nice to see you."

"Hi, Bella." They hugged shoulders. Jack was huge, and had to bend low to kiss her on the cheek. "Where's the old man, eh?"

My father came in from the front balcony where he'd been sitting on one of our vinyl folding chairs scribbling on a pad of graph paper. He had on his brown, backless slippers, and they slapped rhythmically as he walked up to Jack.

"How're you doing, you old sonuvagun," Jack said.

"Not bad, not bad at all," my father answered, shaking his hand and then leading him through the living room to the balcony. He yanked open another chair for Jack and set it beside him. Jack pulled out a cigarette and lit it despite the breeze, while my father smoked a cigar. He only smoked cigars when out on the balcony, or during hockey games, and the smell coming in through the screen door reminded me of the play-offs the previous month. We'd watched the Canadiens play Toronto on our old black-and-white TV, and I'd yearned for a colour TV so that I could see the teams' uniforms properly.

"Go play in your room, or outside," my mother told me.

"But I want to watch TV," I said. I didn't want to get too far from where the excitement was.

"Fine, but only if you keep the sound down and don't bother your father."

I knew that the only things on were boring nature programs and religious shows, but I kept turning the dial anyway, trying to catch what was being said outside. My father and Jack were deep in serious, and then joking, conversation. Jack was one of the few people my parents knew who, like them, spoke without an accent. He drove a Citroën, a weird-looking foreign car with rear fenders that almost covered the wheels completely. I'd visited his apartment once—it was in a modern high-rise overlooking Côte Des Neiges, and had struck me as the kind of place we'd all be living in some day: bright, fresh-looking, without the clutter of my own or my relatives' homes. I wanted to live that way, beyond the old-fashioned ugliness I associated with my grandparents. It was the world depicted in *The Boys' Book of Science Fiction Stories* and on *Star Trek*: the lines geometrical and the surfaces featureless and polished clean.

They talked for over an hour, but I didn't learn anything from my eavesdropping. Jack stayed for supper, and when my sister returned from playing at a friend's house he greeted her by calling her princess, which I thought hilarious. Over boiled chicken, mashed potatoes, and Niblets corn my father finally told us what they'd been discussing for so long.

"We're going to start a business," he said, smiling more broadly than I'd ever seen him.

My mother wiped the corner of her mouth carefully. "A business?" she asked, eyes narrowing. "What kind of business?"

"Well, Jack knows the people down at Expo, and we could deal in some of the souvenirs, but for collectors."

"Yeah," Jack said. "Some of them are saying the site will be used next year, too; they're not just going to tear it all down. They might have an exhibition every year, and we'll be right there."

My mother looked at my father strangely. "What do you know about selling?"

"I don't have to know. Jack's the salesman. He'll teach me whatever I need to know." He lowered his knife and fork and spread out his hands. "I don't have to work for someone else my whole life, you know. I can do better than Lorenz; he treats me like I don't know what I'm talking about, anyway." My father was a bookkeeper and was always complaining about his boss ignoring his advice, paying him too little (and sometimes not on time). This was a chance for my father to escape all that, and I didn't understand why my mother could object. "Look, if this works out we'll be able to buy a house like I've been promising. We won't have to always worry about the next pay-cheque, or if Lorenz suddenly decides he doesn't like the way I keep the books."

My mother remained silent.

"A chance like this doesn't come every day, Bella," Jack said.

"Why should I always have to worry about money all the

time?" my father said. "I'm tired of being someone else's slave."

My mother's eyes widened. "You're going to quit your job?"

"No, I don't have to. Not right away. We'll see how it goes."

It sounded fantastic. Finally we'd have enough money for anything we wanted. I wouldn't have to listen to my parents arguing over what they could and couldn't afford. We'd be able to move into a real house, as my parents had been promising for years, and I'd get my own room at last. We'd all have anything we wanted. Couldn't my mother see that?

She shrugged. "Do it if that's what you think's best."

"That's what I think's best," my father replied.

Jack didn't stay long after supper, and my parents didn't say much to each other after he left. I stood on the balcony waving down to him as he got into his ultramodern streamlined car, which looked like it could fly if only the rounded tail contained rockets. He waved back up at me before driving off, elbow stuck out the driver-side window. I watched our stupid old TV and thought that at last we'd get a new, colour one.

That night I couldn't sleep; I imagined the changes our family would finally undergo. It was about time my parents stopped having to count every penny. My door was open just a little, to let in some of the light from the hall, and through it I heard my parents arguing.


A few days later I came home from school to find a brown cardboard box sitting in the middle of our living room. *New East Industries* and *Hong Kong* were printed in thick, black letters on all sides.

"Is that the stuff Dad's going to sell?" I asked my mother.

"I guess so. What happened in school today?"

I told her about getting an E (for Excellent) in spelling again; I hadn't gotten as low as a VG+ in weeks. I also told her about the new reading system we were trying out called SRA, though I didn't know what that stood for. Long passages were printed on coloured plastic sheets, and we had to answer the questions at the end.

"I never heard of such a thing."

"Neither did I." The sheets came in a stiff box and were ordered by colour. It was all very complicated, but of course my teacher knew what she was doing, even if she didn't seem very sure about the instruction card that came with the set. She'd described it as a modular system, which sounded like "modern" and seemed new and scientific.

When my father came home he headed for the box as soon as he'd kissed my mother, smiled as he hefted it, then got the scissors from the kitchen. With one arm of the scissors he sliced the wide cellophane tape and pulled the top flaps apart. Inside was an amazing array of multi-coloured objects in plastic bags: ashtrays, toy bugles, pennants, each with the word "Montréal" printed in blue.

There was so little inside the box that I thought my father could have no problem selling everything; it would be a cinch to get our house and all the rest. I reached in to pull out a white ashtray and my father pushed my hand away. "Don't touch, Lar. These are samples."

"Oh."

My sister sat on the floor next to the box. "You're going to sell all of these?"

"I hope so." He picked up some of the samples and looked at them closely, then put everything down again and tried to push the flaps back in place. "Come on; let's have supper." One of the flaps rose of its own accord, poking up in mid-air.

"Is that stuff any good?" my mother asked as she spooned cold peas onto our plates.

"It costs practically nothing but we can sell it high," my father told her. "That's the secret. People will buy it because it's Expo."

My mother shrugged. "I hope you're right." Then she asked Sheila and me more questions about school, never mentioning the box and its contents again. I thought that was pretty strange, considering how important the new business would be to us. Jack came by later and picked up the box, and my father followed him downstairs to talk. My mother stood at the sink doing the dishes, and even though she answered me whenever I asked her a question, or smiled when I told her some piece of news, I knew she wasn't listening, not the way she normally did.

For some reason I heard very little about the new business over the next few weeks. My father earned a little extra money doing bookkeeping for other people besides his bosses, and on Saturdays and some evenings he continued to disappear into the office he'd set up in the spare bedroom. The office was out of bounds to Sheila and me, but we both coveted it. We still shared a room, and I was sure he'd drop the bookkeeping clients and give the room to one of us. But he behaved as if nothing had changed, and my brief hope that I'd finally get my own room faded.

It was June; school would end soon, Expo was about to open, but above all we'd be able to watch my father's new business get going and the money start rolling in. Sometimes my father talked about it at the table. My mother seemed to be only half-listening as he told her about the contacts Jack had made, and how they were both sure the sales would be great.

"They're not going to just let the place fall apart," he said. "Tourists will be coming here for years. Like Drapeau said, it's going to put Montréal on the map."

"You're probably right," my mother said. I wanted her to mean it; I was mad at her for just saying it.

"I'm not doing this for myself, you know." My father took a slice of challah and used it to wipe his plate clean of gravy. "It's for the whole family. Why should we always rent? Why should we always live in a place like this?"

"I like it here," Sheila said. "I don't want to move."

"Don't you want to live in your own house?" my father asked.

She shrugged and said, "I guess so."

I knew what she meant; I didn't want to move, either. This was my neighbourhood, where all my friends were, where my school was. But I also knew that things would be so much better if the tourists kept coming the way Jack and my father said. And they couldn't be wrong.

"Look, let's just eat." My mother's "let's not discuss this any more" tone always worked. "What's done is done."

After dinner I went to my room to read one of my Tom Swift, Jr. books, but my sister was playing one of her rock music 78s on my parents' old record player, the one they gave her after buying the hi-fi. To escape the noise I sat out on the back balcony, watching the shadows lengthen in the yard below.

When Expo opened we watched the ceremony on the news. Huge crowds of people stood listening as Mayor Drapeau and Prime Minister Pearson made speeches. The camera panned around to show all the fantastic pavilions, especially the American geodesic dome. This was what our cities would look like soon; I figured it wouldn't be more than five years before all of Montréal was under a dome just like it.

But it was another two weeks before I got to see those pavilions in person. My father had some business to do at Expo anyway, and so we made a family outing of it. We drove down very early Saturday morning, much to my dismay (summers were for sleeping in), but the traffic was still bad near the site. The parking lot was divided into sections, each represented by different animals. We parked in the hippo section. The TV reports had made the whole site seem nice and compact, but as we walked toward the admission gate to Ile Notre Dame I saw the pavilions I recognized from TV stretching out for what seemed like miles. Behind us was the Montréal skyline, the grey and white office towers hazy and dreamlike over the river.

My father got out the map with the Sunoco and Pepsi-Cola logos on it, and we made our way to the main gate past the Autostade. We joined an absolutely huge lineup at the turnstiles, where my father flashed the passport. Once we were finally through we followed the signs to the Expo-Express train, which we would take all the way down to Ile Notre Dame where most of the pavilions were, especially Canada and Israel. Thousands of other people, it seemed, jammed into the train with us, but we made sure to get on the front car and stand near the window where we could see as much as possible.

The train took us by Habitat '67, with its blocks stuck together at wild angles like something I might have made out of Lego; I vowed to live there some day if I could. We then crossed over a bridge, and in the distance I caught my first look at the geodesic dome, glinting in the hazy sunlight. I stared in wonder out the train window, ignoring the press of people around me, as I watched it rise in the distance. The closer it came the more I felt as if I'd been transported fifty or a hundred years into the future and imagined seeing spaceships soaring over it. The other pavilions around it were smaller but colourful, geometric, fresh-looking.

We crossed another bridge, steering towards the tall white tower of the British pavilion and the silver and glass French pavilion. Every pavilion below us was a different shape, but none looked like any building I'd ever seen before. The train pulled into the Ile Notre Dame station and we followed most of the people out, then down into the midst of Expo.

It was all so crowded we could barely move. The streets between the pavilions were filled with streams of people going both ways, which parted only to let La Balade—the roofless tour train on wheels—go by. There was so much I wanted to see, like the Bell Pavilion with its movie that surrounded you and something called The Labyrinth which sounded interesting, but the lineups at almost every pavilion were enormous. We ended up walking from one end of Ile Notre Dame to the other before finally sitting down outside the Canada pavilion. I didn't mind too much not getting into the pavilions because I relished just moving between all those huge structures that were so different in colour and size and especially shape. We did manage to visit the India, Iran, and Mexico pavilions, where the lineups weren't bad; they smelled of new carpet, and had multi-media displays with slides and taped voices. I didn't understand all of it, but that my image of India as a place full of starving people was confirmed. I kept thinking of the Unitarian Service Committee commercials, and that woman with the strong accent begging for money. At the door of each pavilion a young woman in uniform took our passports and stamped them. My mother made some joke about it being a small world, and my sister kept saying she wanted to ride the mini-rail, but no one wanted to wait an hour or two in line to get on.

Outside the pavilions the smell of French fries was everywhere, except for near the West Germany and Austria pavilions which smelled of beer. Bands and clowns manoeuvered through the crowds, but we often missed seeing them because of people getting in our way or because we were headed in a different direction. We ate hot dogs dripping with mustard at one of the stands (where we also had to wait in line) and drank

Allan Weiss

Coke in cups almost entirely filled with ice. I couldn't get over the triangular garbage cans, or the glass-domed phone booths, or the stick-figure signs for the washrooms. Near the end of the day we headed for La Ronde. The line for The Gyratron was even longer than the one at the Bell Pavilion, and I was too tired to wait even if my parents had been ready to take me.

"We'll be coming back again anyway," my father said. While my mother, Sheila, and I were at the Iran pavilion he'd gone off to do some work; I thought it was a shame that he'd missed it, but when he looked at the stamps on our passports he seemed happy enough. I wanted to hear how many souvenirs he'd sold, but he never said.

We walked back toward the hippo lot through crowds that didn't seem any smaller; in fact, there were still lineups at the pavilions I most wanted to go to. But we did manage to visit the Israel pavilion, which was not too hard to get into, and I stood looking over the diorama of Jerusalem, guarded by giant masks of people from the Bible. The blue carpet, the dark walls, and the colourful displays were both stifling and exhilarating; all of it seemed so new—even the city that I thought would still look ancient.

We went back to Expo a few times that summer, but not nearly as often as I thought we would. We eventually got to visit the Bell pavilion and see the 360° movie with its Mountie charge and helicopter flight over the Rockies; we took the minirail through the American pavilion and then finally managed to get in to see it properly, but all they'd put inside that wonderful dome was a bunch of giant pictures. We saw some of the theme pavilions but I didn't understand much of what their movies and slides showed; and I couldn't stop staring at the huge pines in the Western Provinces pavilion.

But we never did ride the Gyratron, and we kept missing

seeing the dragon at the Canada pavilion raise its head and snort fire.

More than anything, I wanted to hear about the business. I kept waiting for my father to talk about it, to tell us about its progress and how much money he was making. I asked him about it sometimes, but didn't get much of an answer. It wasn't fair; this was something just as important to me as it was to them, but because I was a kid I wasn't told anything. I wanted what I'd been promised, or at least to know how close we were to it.

Then one hot night when we were all sleeping with our doors open to get a breeze I heard my parents talking in their room. My sister was already asleep; I could hear her breathing evenly behind the sheet she'd strung up on an old clothesline between our beds.

"I told you, Hank," my mother said; "I told you what he was like. You knew."

"Yeah, yeah." Neither my father nor my mother said anything for a while. Then my father said, "It looked right."

"He's got no family; he's got no one, nothing." I'd never heard my mother sound so dismissive about anyone. "What does he care?"

"He cares."

"No, he doesn't. He comes up with these big, fancy shmancy ideas of his all the time."

Again neither said anything for a while. I refused to believe that anything had gone wrong; maybe I was misunderstanding them. I started to doze off. But before I fell asleep I heard my father say, "I know."

A couple of days later Jack came to the house after supper, and he and my father sat in the office with the door closed. *Lost in Space* was on, and even though it was a repeat, and I knew the show wasn't all that good any more, I watched the episode anyway, wanting nothing more than to watch the

Jupiter II in flight through star-specked space. The round lights below the saucer spun, and you could just make out the tiny people (I could tell they were just stiff little models) looking out through the front port, as the silver spaceship crossed the blackness headed for unknown regions of space. Maybe next season they'd come up with better ideas.

Jack and my father came out of the office during the last commercial before the show's cliff-hanger, and I stood watching Jack leave. My father looked very serious, but Jack still seemed the same: loud, with that announcer's voice, and always moving quickly despite his size.

"Hey, no harm in trying, eh, Hank?" he said.

"Yeah."

They shook hands and Jack saw me standing there. "Hey, Sport! See you soon." He feinted poking me in the stomach; I flinched and laughed.

"Bye." I went to the front window and watched him drive his weird-looking car away.

Later that night I looked into my parents' bedroom. My father was in his armchair beside the bed, reading one of his fat Science Fiction Book Club books by the light of the bedside lamp on the nightstand. I'd expected him to look sad, or angry; but he looked no different from all the other times he'd sat in that chair, the fingers of his left hand twirling the curls at the top of his head.


They did keep Expo going for a few years, calling it *Man and His World*, and we even went a couple of times. But people lost interest, especially after they shut down two of the islands and most of the pavilions. It just wasn't the same. The worst thing was when the American pavilion burnt down years later. Instead of a shining glass ball all that stood there was a half-sphere of bent metal girders.

*Lost in Space* was cancelled after 1968, and I was really upset. There were other shows I could watch, though, like *Land of the Giants*. My father bought the *Life* magazine retrospective on 1968, with the Apollo 8 photo of Earth in full colour on the cover. I thought we'd see something that clear and vivid on TV when Apollo 11 landed, but all we got was a hard-to-see, obviously black-and-white picture that didn't even show Armstrong's foot touching the ground. My father sat leaning forward, hands folded, and when Armstrong finally came out of the LEM after that agonizing wait, and lowered himself down the stairs, I saw my father punch his knee lightly. I glanced up and I could see him smiling, eyes bright, almost exactly the way Walter Cronkite looked when the camera switched to him.

"Isn't that something," my father said. I nodded, but he wasn't saying it to me. "Isn't that something," he repeated, I don't remember how many times.

# Envelopes

In the days leading up to my Bar Mitzvah I had a pretty good idea of what to expect. Besides three years of Hebrew School, I'd had a couple of months of Bar Mitzvah lessons from Rabbi Gelman, one of my father's bookkeeping clients. He lived in a small apartment near Plamondon, and every Sunday morning my father drove me there and picked me up an hour and a half later. The luxury of being driven to and from a school almost compensated for giving up my Sunday mornings—even if the only thing on TV worth watching was *Davey and Goliath*. But at least I'd finally see the day I'd prepared for all those years. My day.

We would sit at his marbled grey kitchen table, crammed in between the squat round-cornered refrigerator and the gas stove he kept turning on to heat up the kettle for his coffee. The whole place smelled of something indefinable.

"Every month is another *Haftorah*," he said the first day, drumming on his forehead with the bony fingers of his right hand. He was a small, skinny old man with sunken cheeks and just a fringe of hair around the base of his head.

"A story from the Torah. Some longer than others. You understand?"

I nodded—what was hard to understand about that? The kettle whistled.

"Yours, I have to tell you, is long," he warned as he spooned coffee into his cup and poured in the hot water slowly, as if doing a chemistry experiment. "One of the longest." I knew he was trying to worry me, maybe in order to ensure I'd pay attention, but I refused to be scared. Anyway, since this was my Bar whatever happened was mainly my business. "Your father says you went to Hebrew School?" he asked.

"Yeah."

"Won't be that hard. But you have to sing, you understand?"

I nodded again.

"Nah! We try." He stirred his coffee and took a sip, making a strange face. From the nearby counter piled with papers of various sizes and colours he pulled a small stapled booklet called *Hamaftir*. "This is for October," he said.

When he opened the booklet, I saw on the right-hand page the familiar Hebrew letters with their accompanying vowels, plus a few extra symbols I didn't think meant anything. On the left was an English translation.

"First you do the *brochah*, you understand?"

"Yes." The blessing on the *Haftorah* was, fortunately, pretty short and similar to all the other blessings I'd learned at Hebrew School. "*Baruch atoh Adonai elohaynu . . .*" I read the blessing back to him without making more than a couple of pronunciation mistakes, which he corrected—annoyingly—before I had a chance to correct myself.

"Good, good. We do again next week." Then he turned the page, said, "Nah!" and pointed to the Hebrew text. "*V'ishah achat minshay vnay hanve'em el-Elisha laimor . . .*" he sang, then motioned to me to repeat after him. I copied the modulations of his voice, while he stared at the page and cocked his head in my direction. I had no idea what I was singing, but I had little trouble reading what his thin finger pointed to, and the "tune" seemed to be nothing more than an alternation of going up very high and coming down very low. It would be a cinch.

I knew that my mother would be relieved that I was having no trouble with my Bar Mitzvah lessons. She'd spent the past three years making sure I was prepared for my Bar. Her whole point in sending me to Hebrew School was so that I learned enough of the language to get through the ceremony, even though I kept telling her that they weren't teaching us much vocabulary. We spent most of our time practising to sound out the letters and reviewing for the hundredth time the origins of every holiday. Even then, we weren't told much about these events, such as when they occurred; Esther, Judah Maccabee, and Moses could have been around at the same time, for all I knew. We learned only enough Hebrew to translate simple sentences like "Mother gives food to Dan," but that didn't seem to matter to my mother. Or me. All I needed to know was how to distinguish one letter from another so that I could handle my part of the Bar Mitzvah ceremony.

During that summer and fall my mother arranged everything else without consulting me about any of it. She made calls to caterers, florists, and relatives, and booked a synagogue on De Vimy, for some reason, even though none of us had ever gone there; it was near where we used to live, before moving to our new house in Ville St. Laurent, so at least my old friends would have no trouble getting there. She came home one day with a stack of stationery with my name on it: invitations, envelopes, reply cards, and so on. I thought I'd be able to decide whom to invite, but I only got to make a list of my best friends. At least my mother allowed me to fold the invitations, and address the envelopes to my friends (she wouldn't trust me with the others). I didn't know how we could afford the rich-looking stationery, with its raised, shiny black letters on thick, grey paper, but this was a pretty important day for me, and I was glad to see my parents going all out for it. I'd be the centre of attention, more than on any other birthday, and probably get all kinds of presents. My friend Howard Cohen told me after his Bar that he'd gotten over a thousand dollars from his relatives! I'd chipped in with Wayne Fischman to give him a model kit of a Formula One race car.

As my lessons continued I knew things would go well. I realized quickly that those strange symbols under the letters were actually musical notes of some kind, and I could antici-pate when I'd have to raise and lower the pitch of my voice. Rabbi Gelman put ragged pencil marks between the passages I was to learn each week and sent me home with a record of a cantor singing my *Haftorah*. Every week the pencilled passage grew longer, until I was doing almost half a page a week.

"You'll do fine," Rabbi Gelman said one day. "But you shouldn't get nervous, you understand?"

By now I knew better than to respond every time he ended his sentence that way. I stared at the page in front of us, smelling the coffee in the cup he held between his hands, wait-ing for him to finish so we could go on.

"Everyone will be listening, the whole shul, but they're used to Bar Mitzvahs making mistakes. But not too many, you understand? You do it like you do it here, don't even think about who's listening."

Watching Howard do his Bar I'd thought it incredible that anyone could stand up there in front of everybody and sing. His cracking voice had been barely audible, and he backtracked a few times, much to the obvious impatience of the men *dav-ening* in the front row. Afterwards Howard told me that he'd been too nervous to think about what he was doing, and really did forget he had an audience after a while. I knew if I could survive that, everything would be fine; the Bar would go the way it was supposed to.

Rabbi Gelman insisted we go over and over the lines, getting the tune and the pronunciation right. I gritted my teeth and sang the same words for the hundredth time. Again, this was my Bar Mitzvah, and even if I forgot one or two lines it was my problem, no one else's.

I also didn't enjoy putting on the *tefillin*. I had to wrap the leather straps around my finger and arm exactly so many times, but Rabbi Gelman never explained what they were for or what they meant. The boy pictured in *Hamaftir* managed to space out the coils around his arm much better than I could ever hope to. Since *tefillin* are only worn on weekdays I figured the whole process was a waste of time; I couldn't imagine when I'd be in shul on a weekday. Fortunately, Rabbi Gelman didn't spend too much time on them.


On the day of my Bar Mitzvah my father insisted we get down to the shul very early—with at least an hour to spare. My mother had bought me a new suit at Oglivy's, and I spent much of the morning staring at myself in the hall mirror, amazed at how I looked. My father stood behind me tying and retying my tie with trembling hands, trying to get it to stop hanging below my belt buckle. "I'm not used to this . . ." he kept saying apologetically. I'd worn my old suit, with its tight too-short sleeves, to Howard's Bar, and marvelled to see myself in one that actually fit. I was reminded, for some reason, of those pictures in my Grade One reader that showed a man as someone in just this sort of blue suit, white shirt, and tie. Apart from the fact the shirt collar was choking me, I felt very impressive.

"Have you got your yarmulke?" my mother asked, for

about the tenth time that morning. She looked bizarre in her whitish powder, red lipstick, blue eyeshadow, and shiny blue dress; I could smell nothing but perfume when she stood close enough to check my hair again. Even my sister, who was still in her room getting some last minute stuff for her purse, looked like something out of a magazine. Sort of—underneath it all she was still my sister.

I pulled the yarmulke out of my inside breast pocket (the only pocket worth using on a suit, as far as I was concerned) and showed it to my mother. "Yeah, here," I said, yet again, with what was left of my patience. It was a blue velvet one with my name and the date of my Bar in gold letters on the silk lining. At least, I thought it was silk.

"Keep that pocket empty for all the envelopes you'll be getting," she said. "With the presents."

"Okay." Presents? In envelopes?

"When someone gives you the present say "thank you" and put it away; don't look at it till after the Bar Mitzvah." She touched the side of her mouth, thought for a bit, then opened her purse and pulled out the *Hamaftir*, to reassure me and herself that it was actually still in there. "Have you got your speech?" she asked. I rolled my eyes, but checked my pocket anyway. My speech? As if I'd written it, not my father.

"Come on, let's go!" my father called, already out the door. He was starting to gain weight at the time, and we could hear him puffing slightly as he made his way down the front stairs.

"Sheila!" my mother yelled.

"Yeah!" my sister replied from her room. We all had to wait—my father fuming, my mother fussing with the angle of my tie—until she came clopping out of her room in her low heels.

We first drove to pick up my grandmother, who was, according to plan, supposed to be waiting downstairs for us. But she wasn't there, and after waiting tight-lipped for five or ten minutes my father told my mother, "Look, go up and get her. We're going to be late."

"Relax, Hank," my mother said, although she really seemed to be more nervous than him. She went into the apartment building lobby just as Bubby was coming out of the elevator and helped her through the doors. My father kept looking at his watch, occasionally shaking his head while Bubby negotiated the apartment building stairs and then the short walk.

"She goes crazy for everything to go right . . ." my father began, then stopped himself long before my mother and grandmother were close enough to hear. My sister squeezed up against me as my mother lowered herself into the car and Bubby grunted her way into the front seat.

The foyer of the synagogue was already full by the time we got there, and I was introduced to relatives I barely knew or didn't know at all. We had family in Chicago and New York, and many of my American aunts and uncles were in town. I couldn't keep track of their names and had no idea how they were related to me, but it didn't seem to matter; after I was presented to Aunt So-and-So or Uncle Such-and-Such the grownups ignored me completely and talked to each other. It was ridiculous. After all, this was my Bar Mitzvah, and I was supposed to be the main focus of attention. Occasionally I saw kids my own age, but didn't recognize them or—since they were girls—didn't want to know them. I couldn't see any of my friends in that mob.

When it was time to go in my father put his arm around my shoulders and guided me to our seats near the front. My mother handed me my book. "Are you nervous?" she asked worriedly, as if my saying "Yes!" would have made her cancel the Bar. I just shrugged. She smiled, pressed her palm against the side of my face (which made me cringe) and left to join the other women.

People had already taken their seats, and as I walked down the aisle the relatives I'd been introduced to plus many more tugged at me or patted my arm and smiled.

"Oy, he looks so handsome."

"Go get 'em, Sport."

"He's thirteen? He looks thirty-five."

My cousin Ruth sat hunched over because of her bad back; as always, she looked as if she were mad about something. Uncle Nat, her father, sat by the aisle, and as I walked by he smiled at me through his bad teeth. I expected to hear his harsh voice but he remained silent. Beside him was Ruth's brother David, wearing a mod suit with bizarre wide lapels. Uncle Moishe from Ottawa was sitting next to David, trying to get comfortable on the hard wooden pew. Away in the back was a group of my mother's friends from the B'nai Brith; even from here you could hear their voices as they interrupted and talked over each other.

Just as I was sitting down Howard came up from behind me and tapped me hard on the shoulder. "Hey!"

"Hi. When'd you get here?"

"Just now."

"Who else is here? Where's Wayne? Did you see him?"

Howard shrugged. "No."

My mother had limited the number of friends I could invite, which made no sense at all to me. After all, this was my birthday party, in a way, but according to her we had to fit my friends in after all the relatives I didn't know were included. Jeffrey Gold, Wayne Fischman, and Terry Ralston were the only other ones I'd invited. I'd just made friends with Paul Schneider—my only friend at my new school—but too late to put him on the list.

"Gotta go," Howard said. "Don't be scared."

"I'm not."

Facing us up front were three men: a fat man with a neatly trimmed black beard, a very young man who looked no older than David, and Rabbi Gelman. They sat on uncomfortable-looking chairs, patiently watching people file in, and occasionally exchanging a few words. Across the aisle from me was a row of old men with their white satin *talises* draped over their heads: they were the ones I'd really have to impress.

The young man up front—obviously the rabbi of this shul—stood up and tried to get everyone to quiet down. People in the audience also said "Shhhh!" but it took forever to get some of my mother's friends to stop talking. I sat there half-listening to the preliminaries, but mainly looking around. As the rabbi spoke, mostly in Hebrew but sometimes in English, I watched my relatives. Most were paying attention, but some were still trying to whisper. I wanted to go over to them myself and shut them up. Were they planning to talk through my whole *Haftorah?* What were they doing here, anyway?

At last it was my turn to go up and I walked in a daze to the front of the shul. Rabbi Gelman met me at the lectern and helped me open the book. I didn't need to be babied like that, but because I was so nervous I was glad he was there. He pointed to the *brochah* and whispered "Go ahead." My voice trembled, and I felt as if none of this were really happening, that it was a dream. The words began pouring out, smoothly, and my voice held steady as I sang the blessing. The other two men stood up and swayed next to me. At the end, the entire congregation—rabbis, cantor, the whole audience, even the *daveners*—said, "Omain" as if my leading the prayer were perfectly routine.

Rabbi Gelman then turned the page for me and said, "Don't be scared, you understand? Just go ahead."

For a second I stared at the page, having forgotten every single thing he'd taught me. But the squiggles above and below the words jolted me back. I stopped thinking about it and just sang, as if this were just another lesson, and I almost—but not quite—managed to forget about everyone sitting there. I knew they were watching me, maybe hoping I'd make no mistakes or maybe not caring about that.

I knew all eyes were on me but that didn't bother me any more, although I was sure the old men would hate me if I made some error in the words or tune. But even they couldn't bother me all that much. This was my Bar, and like the small tree in my old backyard this ceremony was entirely my own property, my own business.

Near the end I was both relieved and disappointed. I was glad I'd be able to get out of the spotlight soon, but I'd worked so long towards this ceremony and now it was almost over. I sang in full voice right to the end, stretching out the final notes to delay the moment when I'd be told to sit down.

At last Rabbi Gelman tapped me on the shoulder, gave me a satisfied little smile, and I walked back to my seat. The service continued, the cantor crying out his own song in a voice that rang throughout the synagogue.

"That was very good, Lar," my father said when there was a moment of near-silence while everyone prayed under their breaths. "Real good."

Everyone called "Omain!" in response to something the young rabbi said—not that I was listening—and the congregation started up out of the seats. Many headed in my direction.

"You sang beautifully," Aunt Tillie said.

"Very nice, very nice," someone else behind her added.

"You gonna be a cantor when you grow up, kid?"

"Nice, I've never heard so nice."

"Here's a little something, doll."

"Don't spend it all in one place!"

The woman gave me a long, thin envelope, and I slid it into my inside pocket without opening it, as my mother had said to.

"Such a lovely voice," the woman concluded before disappearing into the mob.

My mother came up, her smile strange under the makeup. It was her sad-happy smile that had always been painful for me to look at. She gave me a tight hug, and I shyly returned it. "You did a terrific job," she said, then moved back, still holding my shoulders and looking as if she would cry at any moment. I hoped my friends hadn't seen any of this.

We moved as a tightly packed crowd out of the shul proper and down some winding stairs into a hall where tables had been set up and women in maids' uniforms rushed around straightening out cutlery or flower centrepieces. My father brought my sister and me to the head table while my mother went to get Bubby, who was somewhere behind us talking to relatives.

I was almost as nervous going up the step to the head table as I'd been in the shul, and was sure everyone in the room was watching my every move. But when my father led me to my seat I looked up and saw all my relatives talking to each other. The head table stretched into the distance on both sides; at the far right end sat Rabbi Gelman, wearing a dark suit that was loose on his small frame; a few wisps of white hair escaped from under his black yarmulke. Just to his left sat my Chicago grandparents, saying nothing as they looked out over the crowd standing around the numbered tables below us. My grandmother's jewels glistened under the bright reception room lights, her huge earrings flashing. Sheila and my parents sat next to me, although my mother was too busy saying "hello" to everyone to stay seated for long. My father kept checking his yarmulke to make sure it was still there and at one point my mother tried to reassure him: "It won't fall off, Hank." As if that would do any good.

On the other side sat Bubby and my Uncle Hi and Aunt Rose. Uncle Hi was my mother's brother, but looked nothing like her; my mother was pretty small, but Uncle Hi was tall, and had a sizeable paunch. He was constantly adjusting his black-rimmed glasses, pinky in air, and always looked sweaty. Aunt Rose probably weighed the same, but was a lot shorter. She was playing with her napkin and talking to everyone within earshot; her head kept moving from right to left as she'd answer a question coming from one side then the other, the whole time pulling her napkin through her left hand. The shul's rabbi—whose name no one bothered to tell me—sat at the far left end of the table. Meanwhile, right in front, a couple of my young cousins were sitting at a table punching each other, until their mother half-heartedly ordered them to stop before returning to her conversation. At a table not far from them sat the Craig family, our next-door neighbours; I thought Mr. Craig looked funny wearing a yarmulke. Their youngest daughter Sherri had gotten up and was wandering around the other tables, most of her right hand stuck firmly inside her mouth. She was greeted by smiles from the grownups and suspicious stares from the kids.

I fingered the thick white tablecloth and waited for the food to arrive. At each setting was a little booklet with gold lettering and a gold tassel. I flicked through mine just to have something to do. No one was paying me any attention, except my sister who was just as bored as I was and said things like: "Look at those babyish jerks" (referring to my cousins) or "Who's he?" I shrugged. Most of these people were complete mysteries to me, even after my mother's earlier introductions. At Howard's Bar, I'd sat at a table near the back with our friends from Bedford School and hadn't noticed just how many relatives get invited to Bar Mitzvahs. Howard, Wayne, Jeffrey, Terry, and a couple of girls were seated by the entrance; Wayne waved at me, and I waved back. They looked odd and very uncomfortable in their blue or grey suits. Jeffrey's tie curved under his lapel and then back out again to rest on the table.

The young rabbi stood up and began coughing lightly, and "Shhhh!" ran around the room again, to no avail when it came to my mother's friends. He led the *brochahs*, but very few people recited with him.

I was starved, and ate quickly: tiny roast chicken, mashed potatoes, some kind of green vegetable I tried and pushed aside, brown soup, challah rolls, and purple wine I tasted just enough of to make me wonder why anyone would drink it. Not the kind of meal I would have picked; I'd had no say about anything. I couldn't have arranged a hall, or done all the invitations, but at least I could have had some say about the food. The maids continued winding their way around the tables, one of them barely stopping in time when some small kid got in the way and almost sent huge trays of well-laden plates flying. I overheard a few of the maids talking to each other and realized they were all French. Uncle Moishe threatened to pinch the bottom of one of them, who flashed him a very brief smile, then rushed off looking very unhappy.

I looked over at my mother, who ate and talked, ate and talked. Sheila ate slowly, pausing occasionally to watch Bubby Teitel play with her jewellery. My Other Grandmother, as I called her, was one of the very few Americans I'd ever seen in real life, and I was sure there was a foreign air about her. I kept expecting her to look critically at things Canadian and say how much better American this or that was. I wouldn't put up with it if she did.

"Hank, I'm telling you it won't fall off. Even if it does, just kiss it and put it back on."

"Moishe still hasn't grown up; look at that, Rose."

"Trudeau's a smart man, don't kid yourself. He's a Pepsi but he's no FLQ. What I want to know is, is he still a Communist?"

"Stop playing with that thing, Hank! You're messing up your hair."

My mother actually turned to me. "Are you having fun, dear?"

"Yeah." But I made sure it wasn't an enthusiastic "Yeah". She smiled lightly and turned away again, hunching across the table to talk to Uncle Stan, who had three gold teeth spaced along his upper set.

"Lawrence," my sister said, jabbing me in the ribs. She was in her pestering mode.

"Ow! What?"

"Who is he?"

"Who?"

"That guy, the one at Table 9."

I tried to pick out the one she meant but it was impossible to zero in on one stranger out of dozens. The only one who stuck out at that table was a middle-aged, almost-bald man dressed in a burgundy sport jacket and brown checked pants. I watched him for a bit, noticing that he seemed to be drinking more wine than anyone else. "Him?" I asked, pointing, although I could have been aiming my finger at any of a number of people.

But she nodded. "Yeah, him. I don't recognize him."

"Neither do I. But I don't recognize most of the people here."

"I know most of our relatives but not him."

"Probably from the States," I suggested as I watched him down his wine. The one thing we did know about Americans, from our trips to Plattsburgh and rare visits from American relatives, was that they did everything in excess.

I left most of my vegetables aside—peas with dimples in them, stuff that looked like brains and tasted the way brains probably did—and waited for the dessert. During the lull, relatives and family friends came around the head table and shook hands or kissed me on the cheek, then handed me their envelopes.

"Keep it for your education."

"Don't spend it all in one place."

"Use it in good health."

By now my pocket was starting to bulge, so I slid the pile to my mother who stuffed them into her tiny purse.

Dessert was orange sherbert, which looked a lot creamier than it was. But I liked it, and ate it quickly, before it became a pale yellow sauce in the dish. I knew better than to ask for seconds—they probably had exactly one serving per person, no extras. The young rabbi stood up again, and once more everyone shushed everyone else without much success. Even after he began addressing everyone, a couple of women got in a few words to each other, and some people nearby turned to give them looks.

"My friends," the rabbi said, "it is always a joyous occasion when a young boy reaches . . ."

I watched the uniformed women move between the tables with huge chrome pots of coffee.

" . . . because as it says in the Torah . . ." I felt my stomach start to churn, as it had before I went up to do my *Haftorah*, and I wanted to go sit with my friends. I knew what it was time for. " . . . in our society thirteen is usually an unlucky number, but . . ."

By now many people had stopped listening to him; they were whispering to each other, or looking around the room the way I was.

"And now, our Bar Mitzvah would like to say a few words."

I stood up and drew the speech out of my inside pocket. Not my speech—Dad's speech, the one he'd composed and carefully printed on a blank page torn from one of his order books. This was my chance. I unfolded the paper and pretended to look at the words. Even though I wasn't a little kid any more, I somehow believed that words would come to me, flow from some magic place inside. My heart pounded and I broke out in a chilling sweat. I could barely speak.

"Thank you for coming to my Bar Mitzvah," I said. "This . . . I have . . ."

I glanced up and saw everybody staring at me. Out of the corner of my eye I saw my father shift in his seat. And I realized that I couldn't do it, for a thousand reasons. The words weren't there, and even if they were I'd only make people mad. I had to do what I was supposed to do, for my sake and everyone else's.

I took a deep breath and read out my father's words, telling everyone how glad I was they'd come to help me share this important day, especially the people from out of town, and how I'd do my best to continue to make my parents, grandparents, and all the rest proud of me. And in spite of everything I was actually glad to have the words laid out for me. That made so many things easier.

"It has been a wonderful day for me," I said in a cracking voice, "and I hope all of you—"

"I want it!" Sherri Craig whined as she reached for the huge centrepiece in the middle of the table. When I looked back at my speech I lost my place, and it felt like hours before I found it again.

"—and I hope all of you will remember this day as I most certainly will for all my life."

"CAN'T I HAVE ONE FLOWER?"

My father's words got a big round of applause, then I sat down, trying to slow my heartbeat. The rabbi stood and led the blessings on the meal printed in the white-and-gold booklets.

"I WANT IT!"

"Hank, should I get out a bobby pin for it?"

"No, leave me alone."

"Stanfield couldn't win an election if he was the only one running. He puts people to sleep."

"Yeah, can you imagine Trudeau meeting Nixon? Oy! They'd be at each other's throats in no time."

"Nixon'll get out of Vietnam in two years. Mark my words."

"No way!"

I watched with joy as my friends wended their way toward the head table. Howard led the others—he was the expert, being the only one who'd already had his Bar. People were now standing by their tables stretching, and the bartender in the short white jacket was setting up his bottles on the counter of the little bar set up against the left-hand wall. Rabbi Gelman maneuvered through traffic to stand over me and say: "Congratulations and many years of happiness."

"Thank you."

"You were an excellent student. I have to go now, you understand?"

"I understand."

I stood up and went over to meet Howard and the others. Terry, like the Craigs, looked weird standing in a shul in a yarmulke, although he did look Jewish in a way, with his curly hair and glasses.

"Hey, Lawrence, not a bad Bar," Howard said. "Almost as good as mine, eh?"

"Better."

"Speaking of which . . ." Jeffrey began mysteriously, then he and Wayne looked over at the bar, which was now in full operation. "Want to get a whiskey sour?" Wayne nodded and the two disappeared.

"See you!" Howard said, and started to run after them. "Oh, yeah, here's your card." He gave me a wide, thick envelope before disappearing.

Now relatives came in fast and furious, handing me envelopes and wishing me well. Each had his or her own line: "Very nice Bar Mitzvah, Lawrence. *Kenahora*. You should only be well." One woman went into a long spiel about how she had once baby-sat me. "I changed your diaper, and now look at you! A *mensch!*" she concluded, before giving me the envelope. And as soon as Uncle or Aunt or Mr. or Mrs. Whoever gave me the envelope, he or she rushed off to talk to some other grownup.

One of my mother's friends from the B'nai Brith pushed her way through the crowd toward me, leading one of the girls who had been sitting in the back with my friends. "You remember me, honey?" the woman asked. I nodded uncertainly. "Your mother's friend, Selma."

"Oh, yeah." I could never keep those names straight. Sometimes the whole bunch would come over for a "meeting" at our house, which consisted mainly of playing Rumoli and talking.

"This is my daughter, Rhonda."

Rhonda was one of the prettiest girls I'd ever seen, even better-looking than Charlene Reynolds at school, although that was mainly because of her dress. It was like a princess' dress in our old school readers, with puffy, sheer shoulders and sleeves and a lace collar. She didn't say anything more than "Hi" before asking her mother if they could go back to their table.

"Don't you want to make friends?"

"Mom!" Rhonda whined, rolling her eyes almost exactly the way my sister did when something bothered her.

"Be nice!" Selma hissed, moving over to where some other B'nai Brith members were standing.

"You did a really good job with the Bar Mitzvah," Rhonda said. She wore a large plastic barrette over her left ear that was a marvellous shade of light blue. Lavender or something. I kept glancing at it.

"Thanks."

"My mother said I should give you this." She searched through her little white purse and pulled out an envelope. Her hands were tiny. She wore white leotards that were baggy in a couple of places, and shoes with not very high heels. I couldn't say anything. "Here."

"Thanks."

We stood silently for a couple of minutes before she ran off to be with her mother; I kept thinking about those small hands.

Uncle Moishe stepped up, with Aunt Pearl—a woman only slightly bigger than me—clutching his arm. "Hey, Larry, you old son of a b . . . gun!" He laughed at something. Aunt Pearl smiled apologetically to me. Uncle Moishe lived in Ottawa, and we very seldom saw him; he was fatter every visit. "Here's your top secret assignment," he said, trying to jam the envelope in my full pocket. "Don't let the enemy catch you or they'll cut off your . . . uh, supplies!"

"Moishe!" Aunt Pearl screeched, but then she laughed, too. To me, she said gently: "You sang so nice. Be well, dear."

Howard and my other friends came up from behind just as Uncle Moishe was leaving, Howard and Jeffrey drinking cloudy liquid out of wide, shallow glasses, while Terry and Wayne held ginger ales. Wayne said, "They've got chocolate booze there! Crème de cocoa or something."

"Chocolate booze? No way!"

"Yeah!" And they were off again.

I went back to my mother to unload the envelopes, feeling a bit dazed by all the strangers, all the activity going on around me that had nothing to do with me. Almost everyone in the room had come up to me by this point and given me an envelope—but not the man in the burgundy jacket, who had headed straight for the bar and now stood there talking to the bartender. My mother opened her purse, and as I emptied my pocket I pointed to the guy. If all I was here for was to collect envelopes, at least I shouldn't miss anybody. "Ma, who's he?"

"Who? Your Cousin Barry?"

"No, him. At the end of the bar."

She made a strange face. "Hank? Hank?" My father eventually pulled himself away from Zaidy Teitel and Uncle Nat, and with a look, invited my mother to ask her question. "Who's that man over there, the one in the dark reddish jacket there?"

"Who? That guy?" He studied the man for a couple of seconds. "I thought he was one of your relatives."

"No, I've never seen him before."

My father let out a burst of laughter. "So he's a crasher."

At first my mother looked horrified, then calmed herself, and with a shrug she said in a resigned tone: "Let him enjoy."

"Should I ask him for money?" I ventured, quietly, hoping she'd take it as a joke at worst.

"What, honey?" she said, turning to me with an unreadable expression on her face.

"Nothing." When you're a kid, they assume you don't know very much about anything.

Aunt Clara came up, looking much smaller and older than I remembered, and I walked away from the conversation that developed, keeping my eye on the crasher who was enjoying himself immensely.


In the next hour most of the guests left, the few who had not yet left their envelopes behind slipping them to me as they said good-bye. Cousin Barry, who owned part of a St. Lawrence factory, complimented me on the suit, as if I'd picked it out. Aunt Fay had come up from New Jersey for the Bar and a wedding in Ottawa, and as she was leaving she said: "We don't see your mommy and daddy often enough. Come down and see us!" And for the second time that day she told me I'd sung beautifully.

Howard pulled on his overcoat as he stuffed his face with some little weiners-in-pastry. "I gotta get going."

"Okay. You're coming tonight?" I had to know they'd be there at the reception, to give me relief from the relatives.

"Yeah, of course. We chipped in and got you a great present."

"Present?" Not money? Not a card?

"Yeah. You'll go nuts." He ran out, awkwardly because of his suit, and the others followed. Most yelled, "See you!"

My mother snuck up behind me and put an arm around my shoulders. I wanted to wiggle out from under it but let it stay there. "Lawrence, the appointment at the photographer's is at 3:00 so we'd better get going."

My father went out to get the car, still in debate with Uncle Nat.

"I still say Trudeau's a Communist. He was a card-carrying, sign-painting Commie in the fifties," Uncle Nat asserted, his finger almost in my father's face, "and nothing's changed."

"Practically everyone in the fifties was a card-carrying Communist. So what does that prove?"

"Trudeau's in power, and he's still a Commie!"

"Ahhh . . . !"

My mother got my coat and boots from the coat-check, and I put them on quickly. There were still small pockets of people left in the hall, standing and talking around the messy tables with their gigantic centrepieces. The maids hovered around picking things up, or smoked and engaged in small group conversations of their own. While we waited in the foyer for our car to appear I looked back and saw the crasher holding a tall glass of pale gold liquid as he stood in the middle of the room watching the maids in action. He didn't look at all Jewish, but when he saw me looking at him he raised his glass and yelled *"Mazel tov!"* I smiled back at him as my mother yanked me out to the street.